FOX

SILVER SAINTS MC

FIONA DAVENPORT

FOX

All it took was one look for Kye "Fox" Pearson to know that Dahlia Mackenzie was meant to be his. Then she took off with plans to head to Europe for three months, forcing him to chase her down. Being stranded by a hurricane in a safe house with only one bed was the opening he needed to claim the fiery redhead.

Unfortunately, someone was out for revenge against the club president...and his woman ended up being in the line of fire.

1

DAHLIA

The last thing I expected when I hightailed it to the Iron Rogues compound was to see a man grab my sister and hold a gun to her head. I knew Maverick wouldn't let him take Molly anywhere, no matter the current situation, but I couldn't just stand by and watch what was about to go down. Not when I had the advantage of surprise since everyone's focus was on the wannabe kidnapper and my sister.

The guy was clearly delusional, ranting and raving about how he and Molly belonged together as I crept closer to the action. My breath caught in my throat when he threatened to shoot her if anyone tried to stop them from leaving.

One of the Iron Rogues strode over to Maverick's

side to face off with the intruder. Like most of the bikers I grew up with, he was tall and muscular. He put his intimidating air to good use as he snapped, "Why would you kill her if you love her?"

"If I can't have her, no one can," the guy holding Molly replied with a shrug.

His back was to me, but Maverick and his club brothers' gazes darted toward me and away again. Neither of them looked happy, but I didn't let their irritation stop me from inching forward. My sister's life was on the line, and I wanted to be in the position to help if I got the chance.

"I'm gonna open the gate for you." Maverick's club brother kept a close eye on the gatecrasher as he took a few steps forward.

"You do that. Now, Molly and I are going to walk out to my car, nice and slow. Don't make any sudden moves, or I'll kill her."

If looks could kill, the glare I sent his way at that threat would've dropped him where he stood. Unfortunately, I was so focused on him that I didn't realize Maverick's club brother had used the talk about opening the gate as a way to come up behind me. His hand was over my mouth before I could make a sound, and he quickly dragged me away from the confrontation and to the other side of my Mustang.

Everything moved quickly after I was out of the way. Another club brother threatened, "There's nowhere you can go that we won't track your ass down and feed you a bullet."

Then I heard the distinctive roar of my dad's Harley and squirmed beneath the guy pressing me against the side of my car. With everything going on, I hadn't gotten a good look at him, but that didn't stop my body from having an inappropriate—and surprising—reaction to having his hard body lined up with mine.

I didn't have time to think about it because Maverick used the distraction my dad provided to shoot the wannabe kidnapper. His aim was true, and the guy was thrown backward. He dropped his gun as he went down, but he took Molly with him.

My legs were shaky as my dad roared my sister's name. I held my breath until Dad reached out a hand and helped Molly up, and I didn't see any blood on her.

"Holy hell," I whispered, using the side of my car to slowly get to my feet as Maverick's club brother stepped back.

"Easy, baby."

His deep voice sent a sensual shiver down my spine that was prolonged by the feel of his strong hands gripping my waist. Turning in his hold, I blinked up at him as I took in his salt-and-pepper hair, strong jaw covered with dark scruff, and piercing brown eyes.

As a piercer at Silver Ink—the tattoo shop owned by the Silver Saints, my dad's motorcycle club—I saw a lot of guys with tattoos. I'd never been a fan of neck ink. Not until I saw the black design on his tanned skin above the neckline of his shirt.

It took a moment for the name stitched on the front of his cut to register in my brain. One that I'd heard my dad mention before.

Crap. He wasn't just any Iron Rogue...he was the prez, Fox. Which made my reaction to him even worse.

Not only was my dad here—and angry with me for keeping what Molly had been up to a secret from him—but the man I was lusting over was a club president, just like him. Growing up with my dad in that role, I knew how much was riding on Fox's shoulders. As far back as I could remember, my dad had never struggled with making my mom and us kids a priority, but I knew the same couldn't be said for a lot of other men in the role.

And the Silver Saints were a very different club from the Iron Rogues. They weren't family-oriented the same way, although that might change now that my sister and their VP had hooked up.

Either way, I didn't have time to explore the chemistry between Fox and me. If I wanted to make my getaway to Europe to meet up with some friends for the summer—which was necessary since the last thing I wanted was to sit through a lecture from my dad or be locked in my room like I was still a kid—I needed to head out before the commotion died down and he noticed me. My dad was too observant for my own good, which was a problem when you combined that with how overprotective he was of us girls. I was chomping at the bit to get out from under his thumb for a little while.

Unfortunately, Molly's close call and the guy Maverick just killed to save her would distract him for only so long. The time was now for me to get out of here. Especially since a category 5 hurricane was headed toward the gulf near Tallahassee and my flight was out of Atlanta. The airport was a bit of a drive from Old Bridge, Tennessee, where the Iron Rogues were based, but it was a big enough airport and far enough away that flying from there should throw my dad off my trail, at least for a tiny bit.

Steeling my spine, I stepped away from Fox and

quirked a brow. "Thanks for watching out for me, but I would've been fine."

"Not if you went running straight into the line of fire to try to save your sister," he growled.

I rolled my eyes. "I'd never be that reckless. My dad taught us better than that."

"Then I guess I'll leave the ass chewing to him." He crossed his muscular arms over his broad chest. "I'm sure he's gonna be pissed as fuck that two of his girls were at risk because of that dumb fuck."

"That's a bet that I'm not willing to take." Because I'd be sure to lose, and that was no fun.

"Good call." His gaze flicked toward where Maverick hugged my sister while our dad watched, his fist clenched at his sides. "Doesn't bode well for you that Mac already looks pissed."

Getting out of here without him causing a ruckus would probably be tricky after what just happened with Molly. Everyone was on high alert, and I doubted he would be cool with letting me just drive away. Not when he knew my dad would want to talk if he realized I was here and my disappearing could cause problems between the two clubs.

"It definitely doesn't." I glanced inside my Mustang, and my lips curved into a smile. "Sorry, gotta grab something." Like a flight out of the country.

Fox lifted his chin and headed over to one of his club brothers when he called his name. I took full advantage of his and everyone else's focus being elsewhere and climbed into my car. Luckily, I'd parked closer to the gate, so I was able to pull out right after starting my engine. Then I headed for the airport without looking back...but Fox stayed on my mind during the entire drive.

It was so unfair that I'd found the first man to draw my attention on the same day I was leaving the country to avoid my dad for a few months. My plan was a little extreme, but considering how my dad was, that was the only way it would work. Molly's situation had certainly proven that since it had only taken him a week to find out where she was and who she was with, even with me covering for her. My dad was an amazing parent, but I needed a little space to spread my wings without him looking over my shoulder. I hoped that flying across the ocean would be enough to accomplish that.

I heaved a sigh of relief as I neared the airport without getting a text about my flight being canceled, but I should've known my escape was too good to be true.

2

FOX

Riding down the road like a bat out of hell, I thought about how my life had suddenly veered onto an unknown path. Maverick would be justified if he wanted to give me endless shit about falling for one of the daughters of Mac Mackenzie—the president of the Silver Saints MC. I'd certainly dished it out when my VP had brought home Mac's oldest daughter, Molly.

To be fair, the Silver Saints' reputation was as intimidating as my own club, The Iron Rogues. But everyone feared Mac. He could be a ruthless son of a bitch, though he'd never show that side of himself to his wife and kids, from everything I'd heard about the man.

So when Maverick basically stole Mac's

daughter out from under him, I was fucking livid. We'd built a fragile bond with the Silver Saints, and I had been sure that he would blow it all to hell and start a war. But when it became clear that she was the love of his life, I'd been ready to stand behind him. When I took off an hour ago, I'd been pretty confident that the situation would be resolved with an even stronger alliance. At least, until Mac discovered that I was about to lay claim to his second-oldest club princess, Dahlia.

Despite the shit going down, literally in my front yard, I'd been momentarily stunned when the silver Mustang convertible pulled up and a curvy redhead exited the car. I hadn't been interested in women in a long time, so my swift and violent reaction to her was even more shocking.

She had pale skin with sexy-as-fuck freckles scattered everywhere that my tongue itched to trace. Piercing green eyes, high cheekbones, and full, bitable lips made my cock twitch. Then my eyes dropped to take in her hourglass figure with generous tits, round hips, and thick thighs...my mouth had watered, and my pants had grown overly tight.

She looked a lot like her sister, Molly, and going by her age, I assumed she was Dahlia.

Since we were in the middle of a fucking

standoff with the man stalking Maverick's old lady, I hadn't had much time to appreciate the view. However, I'd known immediately, without a doubt, that this woman was mine.

Mav and I had seen Dahlia creeping up behind the insane man with the gun at the same time. Considering the gun was to his woman's head, I knew he would be in a dilemma about what to do next. He didn't have to make a choice, though. Dahlia belonged to me, and I would take care of her from now on.

After I got her safely behind her car, I made sure to keep her in place and out of the line of fire. Then when the motherfucker was dead, I stupidly left her alone when Blade called my name.

I whipped around at the sound of the Mustang's engine and scowled as I watched it hightail off the compound.

Without another thought, I ran to the garage and climbed onto my Harley, intent on chasing Dahlia down. Although I hadn't seen her yet, I'd overheard her conversation with Molly, when she stated her intention to hide out from her dad in Europe for a few months. That was definitely not happening.

A hurricane was headed up south, causing a fuck ton of rain as I headed out of Tennessee. It had shifted unexpectedly and was headed straight for Atlanta, so if I didn't catch her before she made it on the plane, I'd be stuck waiting out the storm—which would test my patience and probably result in dead bodies—before chasing her around another continent.

In order to avoid those outcomes, I had to make sure I was headed in the right direction. I had a hunch that Dahlia wouldn't use the closest airport if she was on the run. Before I left the compound, I sent a prospect to find one of our enforcers, Deviant. He was our resident computer expert...or as other people liked to call him, hacker. Not as good as Grey —a Silver Saint and a freak of nature—but he came close. I needed him to track down Dahlia's flight information.

Not more than ten minutes into my ride, I had gotten a text on my watch giving me the airport—I'd guessed right, thank fuck—the airline, and the flight number. I hadn't been far behind her, and traffic wasn't as much of an issue for motorcycles as it was for cars, so I did my best to beat her there, even with the rain slowing me down.

My father and Mav's had founded the Iron Rogues, and we'd grown up in the club. Though we'd both worked our way up from prospect, like any other member. Before that, we went our separate ways for a while but remained as close as brothers.

I hadn't always intended to take over for my dad as president. My mom died when I was a teenager, and since she'd always dreamed that I would go to college, I earned a degree in finance from Princeton University. Numbers made more sense to me than people, especially after growing up as the son of an MC prez.

After graduation, I went to work on Wall Street, following the most common path for someone with my IQ and degree. I was known for my skills, but I was also considered wily—which was how I eventually got the moniker "Fox." It didn't take long to put a few million dollars in the bank, at which point I admitted to myself that I was bored as fuck and went back home.

Once I patched, I earned the job as MC treasurer, using my skills to keep the club and its businesses flush. Eventually, Mav returned and patched as well, so when his dad retired and mine followed suit, we were voted into our current roles. It was always useful to throw people off guard when they realized I was wicked smart, a complete nerd, and a bit of a neat freak—Mav's words. But I'd been schooled on martial arts and weapons from a young age, so they would eventually see that I was as lethal and ruthless as any other member of the Iron Rogues.

I sure as fuck hoped my wiliness paid off today because I needed it to snag my woman.

When I drove into the parking lot at the Atlanta airport, I waited near the entrance so I could see Dahlia's car come in. Deviant had let me know she was about ten minutes behind me. While I waited, I called Mav, hoping he'd pick up since it had been several hours from when I left. I figured he would have spent that time in bed with his old lady, especially after almost losing her. But I called anyway.

"Only taking this call to say, what the fuck, Fox?" he growled when he picked up.

"You can give me shit when I get back," I grunted. "Just let me handle the situation with Dahlia first."

I heard a muffled voice in the background and assumed it was Molly, probably asking about her sister. "Want to tell me what the fuck that situation is before I'm forced to kick your ass to make my woman happy?"

"She's mine."

Maverick was silent, accepting my explanation without question. Nothing else needed to be said about that.

"What's the plan?" he asked after a beat.

"Gonna grab her when she arrives and head home. But I'm watching the forecast, and the storm's proving to be unpredictable. If we get delayed, you'll need to come up for air and run shit until I get back. Especially with the Cordell situation so unstable."

Our last job had gone sideways, and we were still dealing with the fallout. Including a crazy asshole who thought he was a key player when really, he was the boss's lap dog.

"Done. Should I tell Lex to make sure the safe house is stocked?"

Like most clubs, we had chapters in other locations, as well as safe houses maintained by prospects in strategic small towns. They also had generators and sat phones in case of an emergency. There was one just over the state line into Tennessee. "Hadn't thought of that option," I mused. "Yeah, have Lex get it ready, just in case."

I wasn't sure if it would be necessary, but taking Dahlia to a small, secluded place for the night—especially if she decided to be stubborn about this whole thing—held merit.

A silver car caught my eye as it approached the ticket machine. "Gotta go. Keep me updated." I hung up without waiting for a response.

Dahlia drove into the covered parking lot, and I watched her search for a spot, then stop a few rows back from the doors to the terminal. I hopped off my hog and jogged toward her, intercepting her a few feet from her car.

"Dahlia," I grunted.

She halted suddenly, her expression a mix of surprise and wariness as she shifted her small suitcase so it would be easily tossed away and turned her key out so it could be used as a weapon. *Good girl.*

"Relax, baby. I'm Fox. The Iron Rogues president."

Her shoulders lost their tension, but her brow furrowed as she cocked her head to the side and studied me curiously. "Um...yeah, I know. Are you going somewhere?" Then her eyes narrowed. "What are you doing here?"

My mouth twitched with the beginnings of a smile, and I winked at her. "I'm here for you, babe."

"P-pardon?" she stuttered, blinking rapidly.

"We need to have a talk."

Dahlia's lips curled down. "Um, okay, but it will have to wait. I have a plane to catch right now, so—"

I shook my head and strode forward, quickly eating up the space between us until we were nearly toe-to-toe. "Now."

"But—"

Even though I'd hoped she would simply agree to leave with me, I knew it was unlikely, so I'd spent the ride coming up with a plan to make it happen. "If you're worried about your dad, I can take care of him," I assured her as my gaze dropped to her plump lips. I was dying to see them wrapped around my cock.

"Take care..." The alarm in her tone caught my attention. "You will ki—"

"Fuck no!" I hurried to clarify. "Shouldn't have put it that way. I meant that I'll make sure you stay hidden from him if you come with me."

"Why would I do that?" she asked, her expression leery. Behind the hesitation, I caught a spark of interest and had to bite back a confident smile.

The moment I'd touched Dahlia earlier that day, I'd felt the electric current between us. When I set her down behind the car, her dilated pupils and flushed cheeks told me she'd felt it too. Some might have chalked it up to the adrenaline of the situation, but when my thumb had brushed over the pulse on her wrist, she'd shivered and licked her lips. It had taken a herculean effort on my part not to feast on her delectable mouth right that second.

I debated whether to be honest or go with the

half-truth I'd thought up on the way here. Ulti-mately, I decided to save the part where I informed her that she was mine and I was keeping her for a time when I had her undivided attention...and it was a fuck of a lot harder for her to run away.

"I'm surprised you'd want to miss your sister's pregnancy. What if there are complications and she needs you?"

Dahlia's mouth fell open, and she gasped. "Molly is pregnant?" she squealed as she clapped her hands and bounced on her toes. If any other chick had done that, I would have rolled my eyes and kept my distance. But Dahlia was cute as fuck when she was giddy. I liked seeing her so carefree and happy, I wanted more of it.

"I didn't think you'd take the chance of missing the birth of your first niece or nephew," I drawled, driving my point home.

"I was only going to be gone for a few months," she objected.

"Unless you got stuck over there for some reason."

The comment caught her off guard, and she contemplated the point I'd made for a minute. "I suppose you're right. I don't want to take the chance, but..." Her gaze shifted over my shoulder toward the airport entrance. "My dad will probably keep me locked up in a tower until I turn thirty, so I'd miss everything anyway."

I rolled my eyes and crossed my arms over my chest, looking down into her gorgeous green pools. "Told you, babe. I'll take care of it."

Her expression was skeptical, and she raised an eyebrow, waiting for me to explain more.

"We'll leave your car here, and my man will make sure you're checked in for your flight. He'll even make the system think they scanned your boarding pass at the gate. We'll leave a trail that will eventually lead right back to the airport." If we let it go cold, Mac would lose his fucking mind and wreak havoc until his little girl was found. "It'll buy you a couple of weeks, at least. Then I'll help you figure out something else."

Dahlia chewed on that for a few seconds, then propped her hand on her hip and asked, "Why would you do this for me?"

Again, I swallowed the impulse to inform her that I take care of what's mine. "Mav's my brother." It was a simple explanation, and I knew it would be enough for Dahlia because she'd grown up in a world where oaths made people more loyal than blood.

I uncrossed my arms and held out my hand.

She bit her bottom lip, and I couldn't stop myself from pulling the plump pink flesh from between her teeth—though I didn't tell her that no one was allowed to bite that lip except me. The touch sent a spark of desire streaking from the spot where our skin met. I watched it flare in her pretty green eyes and smirked when she immediately slid her palm against mine.

Grabbing her suitcase with the other hand, I lifted my chin in the direction of my bike before leading her away from the terminal doors.

I was impressed with how light she'd packed and grateful because her backpack duffel fit into the large tail bag hanging off the back of my bike. The rain had made the spring air muggy, so I hated to make her wear the leathers I'd grabbed before I left the compound. But I would never fuck with her safety. It would be windy once we were on the road, and the protective wear would keep her drier.

Before I could hand her a helmet, she snatched it from my other saddle bag and began to put it on. Chuckling, I batted her hands away and adjusted it before buckling it beneath her chin. So damn adorable. Then I grasped her waist, lifted her, and settled her on my ride.

It was a good thing I'd contacted Mav about the

safe house. By the time we reached it, the rains were torrential, and I could barely see where I was going. We crossed a bridge over a rapidly rising river—the only entrance to the town—and drove for a few more minutes until we reached a small, plain building. It was intentionally nondescript and easily forgettable.

I parked in a shed at the rear and helped Dahlia off the bike before grabbing her bag. Then we made a run for it.

We were soaked to the bone and would both need a hot shower to warm up so we wouldn't get sick. I intended to take full advantage of the opportunity to try to talk Dahlia into sharing the steamy water.

Conserving water and all that shit.

3

DAHLIA

Riding with Fox was a hell of an experience, and not just because we were racing against the storm after it turned in our direction. I had only ever been on the back of my dad's bike before because it was a big deal for a Silver Saint to put a woman on their motorcycle. The feelings being wrapped around Fox's muscular body evoked in me were unfamiliar...and exhilarating.

I hated to give it up, but we couldn't stay on his bike forever with the rain pouring down on us. I didn't ask any questions when he'd pulled off the highway and we drove into a small town. I was just relieved that he had a plan to get us out of the storm. But now that we were safely inside, it struck me that we would be alone for who knew how long. Just the two of us and our intense chemistry.

Looking around to distract myself from the urge to do something wild—like lift his soaking-wet shirt to trace his ink with my tongue—I was stunned by how the inside of the nondescript building didn't match the outside. "What is this place?"

"One of our safe houses."

I let out a low whistle of appreciation to cover my surprise at his answer. Growing up as the daughter of the Silver Saints president, I knew that club business was never shared with outsiders. Hell, information was only given to old ladies when necessary. But here Fox was, giving me the location of one of their safe houses. A place that meant safety and security for the men he'd sworn to protect when he became their president. "My lips are sealed."

"I know, baby." He dropped my backpack duffel on the floor near the door and swept his arm in front of him. "I wouldn't have brought you here if I didn't think you'd keep it to yourself."

I winked at him. "And I wouldn't have abandoned my plans to head to Europe and gotten on the back of your bike instead if I didn't trust you to keep me safe."

"Always."

We'd only just met and had barely talked, but for some reason, I knew deep in my bones that there was a lot of meaning behind that one word. The weight of his promise was thick in the air around us, making me hyper aware of my heart racing.

I was used to seeing life-long romantic relationships forming at breakneck speed, but it was totally different being one of the people falling hard and fast for someone they'd literally just met. A little worried by how quickly my feelings developed, I tossed out another distraction. "If the storm keeps up like this, we'll probably be stuck here until at least tomorrow. Maybe you could give me a tour, and we can check if there are any supplies in the kitchen? I'll probably be starving soon since today didn't go at all the way I'd planned."

That was a huge understatement.

I should've been at Silver Ink all day, but my schedule had been thrown out the window when my mom called to let me know that Cash had stopped at the Iron Rogues compound and saw Molly with Maverick. Of course, he'd immediately called my dad to let him know. The only reason I'd beaten Dad there was because my drive was only two hours while he'd been on a run and was a half day away.

Even with how long it took for word to trickle

down to me that he'd found out and was on his way to Molly, I had just enough time to warn her before making my escape. Which was necessary because Mom had also let me know how pissed Dad was with me for covering for my sister. As if he hadn't taught all of us the importance of loyalty every day of our lives. But unfortunately, my dad was too protective of his girls to use logic when it came to us.

"A quick tour before we shower." His gaze raked down my body, making my nipples pebble. "It'll be the fastest way to warm up before we change into dry clothes."

The image of him, naked with hot water beating down his broad shoulders as I soaped up his broad chest popped into my brain. Feeling my cheeks heat, I ducked my head and mumbled, "Sounds like a good plan to me."

The Iron Rogues safe house was incredible. The living space had two black leather couches and a huge flat-screen television. The kitchen pantry was fully stocked with plenty of dry goods. So much stuff that we could stay for a month without going hungry. The bathroom had a walk-in shower that was more than big enough to fit us both, which had me thinking again about all kinds of things we could do naked. And the bedroom was big...but it had only one bed. A king-sized one with plenty of room to do more than just sleep. With the man whose road name was apt since he was a silver fox with that salt-and-pepper hair of his.

It was a good thing we wouldn't be here for long, or else I'd have a hell of a time stopping myself from climbing him like a monkey. Which I was willing to bet would be an even better ride than being on the back of his bike. Not that I'd know for sure since I had zero experience with men because I'd been waiting until I found a man who I could picture being with forever. It was wild to think that I might've stumbled across him while some asshole was trying to kidnap my sister. And that he chased me all the way to Atlanta to make sure I didn't miss out on her first pregnancy. Which reminded me that I needed to charge my phone so I could give her a call to yell at her for not sharing the news with me herself.

I padded back into the kitchen to get away from the temptation the bed presented, and Fox followed right behind me.

"This place is amazing. I have to admit that I'm surprised by how clean it is, though. Unless somebody needed to be here recently?" I shook my head with a shrug. "Which you can't tell me since it would be club business."

"True," he conceded with a grin. "But that's not the reason. One of the prospects does a safe house run each month, ensuring they are fully stocked and spotless."

I laughed softly. "One of the best parts of the biker lifestyle is having prospects do all the dirty work."

"It sure as fuck has its advantages, but we also have another chapter nearby. Mav checked in with one of their guys to make sure this place was ready for us." He jerked his chin toward the door that he hadn't taken me through during the tour. "But while we're on the topic of club business, only go in there if things go to shit and you need a weapon. That should never fucking happen with me around to protect you, but better safe than sorry."

"Yeah, that's what my dad said when he took Molly and me to the shooting range and self-defense lessons. He wanted us to be ready for anything life threw our way," I explained.

"Always knew your dad was a standup guy. Glad he made sure you can handle a weapon."

Holy crap. Even the way he said "handle"

sounded sexy. It made me picture his dick in my hand instead of a gun.

Fanning myself with my hand while I wondered what it was about Fox that had turned me into a woman with sex on the brain, I peeked into the pantry again. "Looks like I have plenty of options for what to make for dinner tonight and breakfast tomorrow morning before we leave."

"I got some bad news for you, baby." He lifted his hand to wiggle his cell phone. "The river is getting too high, so they're closing the road outta town. Not sure how long we'll be here, but it's definitely gonna be more than one day."

"Oh." I'd never really been one to struggle over what to say, but that was all I could come up with at the moment.

His lips curved into a smirk that showed he knew the impact he had on me, so I was surprised when he didn't call me on it and instead murmured, "You any good in the kitchen, baby?"

I nodded. "Yup."

"That's lucky for me because I'm starving."

The heat in his dark eyes made me think he was talking about more than food. I shivered, and he must've assumed it was because of my wet clothes because he said, "You need to get in a hot shower so you can get warmed up."

"Yeah, that'd be good," I agreed.

"Go on," he suggested, jerking his chin toward the door. "I need to make a call. Club business. But I shouldn't be too long."

"No need to explain, Fox. I get it."

His wording kind of sounded as though he was going to join me in there...which should freak me out. Instead, I wondered how slow I could go while padding over to my bag to bring my stuff into the bedroom.

"Dahlia?"

I paused before disappearing into the bedroom and looked back at him over my shoulder.

"You call me Kye, got it?"

His eyes watched me intensely, and his low and gruff tone sent a shiver down my spine. I nodded, then turned to hide the giant smile that took over my face as I headed to the shower.

4

FOX

I gritted my teeth as I watched Dahlia's sexy hips sway as she walked into the bedroom. I didn't want her out of my sight, but I appreciated that she immediately understood the need for privacy while I handled club shit. As the president of the Iron Rogues, my old lady would need to understand the rules and her role, so it just hammered home the knowledge that Dahlia was fucking perfect for me.

My call was unavoidable, but I was gonna get through that shit as fast as possible. The thought of Dahlia naked, with water running over her curves... fuck. My cock was in danger of punching a hole through my pants.

Quickly, I checked the doors and windows

before setting the alarm, then retrieved the sat phone from the kitchen and dropped onto the couch.

"Seems you survived the weather if you're calling from the safehouse," Maverick muttered when he answered after the third ring, sounding irritated and a little out of breath. I didn't have to guess what he'd been up to...especially since I heard Molly tell him to be patient. I had no desire to know what she was talking about.

"Your concern is touching," I deadpanned.

"You got a hand for that, asshole."

"Is that what Molly said to you right before I called? It would explain the 'fuck you' vibe you're putting off."

Maverick snorted. "Got a real good response to that comment, but I'm not talking about my old lady and sex with anyone. So you'll just have to take my word for it."

"What's happening with the storm?" I asked, not willing to waste any more time trading insults with my VP.

"Lex text you about the bridge?"

"Yeah. Gonna be stuck here for a few days."

"I'm sure you're real broken up about that," Maverick quipped. "Take my advice, spend the time knocking up your woman. It'll be a hell of a lot easier to get Mac to back off if your old lady is pregnant."

I grunted. "Already the plan."

Maverick laughed. "Turns out, we're just like our old men, aren't we?"

I cracked a smile at that. My dad had seen my mom at a drag race. She'd been there with a group of friends, and supposedly, one of them had been her date. But she'd ended up on the back of my dad's bike that night and knocked up with a ring on her finger within a month. Maverick's dad, Rock, had a similar story with his old lady.

"Hear anything else from the DeLucas?" The DeLucas were New York Mafia and one of our best clients. Cordell was an underling, but since he was a second cousin or some shit to the boss, Nic, he'd tried to pull rank with us several times. Demanding to only deal with Mav or me, micromanaging our deliveries, and just being a fucking tool that nearly got him a bullet in the skull every time we worked with him.

The last job was a complete clusterfuck, and eventually, we realized that Cordell had stuck his nose where it didn't belong and fucked everything up.

Maverick practically growled. "I'm gonna kill

that fucker if I ever see him again. You better be
prepared to deal with his ass from now on unless you
want to risk our relationship with the DeLucas."

Sighing, I rubbed the bridge of my nose and
muttered, "I'll call Nic. We've been working together
long enough that I don't think he'll balk at requesting
a new contact." Nic and I had known each other
since my days at Princeton. I hesitated to do business
with a friend, but Nic was as professional and as
lethal as I was. We respected each other, and our
mutual "interests" made the relationship work on
both levels.

Maverick grunted in agreement.

The sound of running water and the shower door
closing caught my attention. I needed to finish my
work shit as fast as possible. "There are no more
meetings scheduled for this week, so for the next few
days, don't call me unless someone is dead or the
club is burning down, got it?"

"Understood."

I hung up and grabbed my cell. The service had
been knocked out, but I had Nic's number stored
in it.

It was almost ten at night in New York, so I knew
his kids would be in bed. But when he wasn't
working late, Nic spent his nights with his wife. And

interrupting that without an emergency could get a man a one-way ticket to the bottom of the East River. So I called his desk phone instead of his cell. If he didn't answer, I'd call Enzo, his number two.

It wasn't necessary, though, because Nic picked up after the first ring. "DeLuca."

"It's Fox."

"*Buonasera*, Kye. I haven't heard from you in a while. I didn't think assigning someone else to your shipments meant we wouldn't talk for months at a time." Nic chuckled, obviously not insulted by my lack of communication. Phones went both ways, and running big organizations took a fuck ton of work.

"Yeah, things have been crazy. I've been meaning to check in."

"I understand." His next words were muffled, sounding like he'd covered the receiver. Then he spoke clearly again. "Gianna said hello and demanded that you and your dad come for a visit."

Gianna—or Anna to everyone except Nic—was his wife. He was well-known for his obsession and being overprotective of his wife, so it said a lot about our friendship that I knew her and their kids so well.

"That might happen sooner than later because we have a situation with Cordell."

"Oh?"

I gave Nic a brief overview of the shit we'd been dealing with, and he cursed.

"Why the fuck are you just now telling me this?" He sounded exasperated rather than angry.

"You're the client, Nic," I drawled sarcastically. "It's my job to meet your needs, not the other way around."

"*Cazzata.* This has been a mutual relationship for a long fucking time, and we've been friends even longer. You should have told me when it first started."

"I figured we'd make it work, but he's made an enemy of my VP, and I can't say my gun wouldn't find its way into his mouth if I ever see him again. Since I don't want to kill your relative—"

Nic scoffed, and my mouth curved in amusement. The Mafia called themselves a "family," and although they also understood that not all true loyalty is born from blood, it still meant more to them than it did in an MC. Cordell was a cousin several levels removed, so he was barely family to Nic.

"I'll handle the *deficiente*," he muttered.

"Thanks. As soon as you pick his replacement, send the details to Maverick. I'll be unavailable for the next few days."

"No more proxies. I'll go back to working with you personally."

"Nic—"

"Your arguments will fall on deaf ears, Kye. So don't waste your breath. Tell your father I said hi. I'll reach out to Maverick and set up a call with him, Enzo, and the both of us, next week."

"Fine." I wasn't going to spend time trying to talk him out of anything when I had the sexiest woman I'd ever seen naked and wet in the next room.

"Also, I apologize for the behavior of my cousin, Kye. He'll be dealt with and instructed to cut all contact with your organization."

"Appreciated. Tell Anna I'll talk to my dad about a visit. Airplanes also fly from New York to Tennessee," I added.

Nic laughed. "But I don't require you to be blindfolded when you come to my home."

I rolled my eyes even though he couldn't see it. "I did that *once*. Just to fuck with you."

"True. But that doesn't mean I'll ever let it go."

"How about you throw me in the trunk for a ride from the airport to your house next time I'm in New York. That's more your style, right?"

"Touché."

"Gotta go," I told him, having run out of patience.

"We'll talk soon, Kye."

After hanging up, I left the phone on the kitchen table and made my way to the bedroom. A smile split my face when I heard the shower still running. I was mostly dried off, and since my body ran at a higher temperature than hers, I hadn't been as bothered by the chill of my wet clothes in the air-conditioning.

However, Dahlia didn't know that. For all she knew, I was about to catch pneumonia. That was why I needed to join her in the shower—or at least that's what I would tell her.

5

DAHLIA

Lingering in the shower had paid off. I was just thinking about stepping out when the bathroom door opened and Fox came in. I stared at him through the foggy glass as he stripped out of his clothes, my breath catching in my throat when I spotted his long, thick dick. It was rock hard, and there was a bead of precome on the tip. I licked my lips, wondering what it tasted like while my breath caught in my throat.

His dark gaze met mine when he slid the shower door open. "You got room in there for me? Conserve some water?"

"Uh-huh." I giggled, finding his excuse hilarious since there was a downpour outside. "I...um...ah, just finished."

"All warmed up?" he asked as he stepped into the shower with me.

"Yup." He was only inches from me. Completely naked. With a hard-on that I assumed was because he felt the chemistry between us the same as I did. "I don't think warm is a strong enough word. More like hot."

"Smoking," he agreed, his gaze dropping to my lips as my tongue glided over the bottom one. "You wanna do something about all this heat?"

I'd held on to my virginity for twenty-four years and had only met Fox a few hours ago, but one thing I'd learned from all the successful relationships I'd seen in the Silver Saints was that when you knew, you knew. "Yes."

A deep groan rumbled up his chest, and he reached around me to turn off the faucet. Then he wrapped one of his hands around my hip and reached out to open the glass door with the other. "C'mon, let's get you dried off so I can get you the much better kind of wet."

Stroking my fingertip over one of the tattoos on his arm, I asked, "I thought you were going to take a shower to get warmed up?"

"Don't need it anymore." His gaze swept down

my body, and he groaned again. "Seeing you was enough to get me so fucking hot, I might spontaneously combust, baby. And no way in hell is our first time fucking gonna be in the shower. I want you all spread out on that big mattress for me where I can explore your fantastic curves."

I thought about telling him this was my first time ever, but then I felt like I was the one who would explode when he started to dry me with the towel. He crouched down, his breath hot against my core as he wiped the water from my legs, and my knees were so weak that I could barely stand by the time he was done. But it turned out that I didn't need to walk because he swept me off my feet and carried me into the bedroom.

After he laid me out on the middle of the mattress, he fisted my hair and tilted my head back to claim my mouth. My lips parted on a gasp, and his tongue swept inside to tangle with mine. The deep kiss stole my breath and made me want more.

Twining my arms around his neck to pull him closer, my back arched off the bed. The movement drew his attention to my breasts.

"When did you get these?" Fox asked gruffly as he broke our kiss, gliding his palms down my chest to palm the rounded globes, his thumbs teasing my nipples.

They puckered at his touch, sending shivers throughout my body.

"My piercings?" I squeaked, my voice betraying me.

"Who else touched these beautiful pink nipples of yours?" he demanded, running his fingers over my already sensitive buds.

"Jealous?" I managed to breathe, though my entire body was on fire. It was hard to concentrate on anything else but where his fingers would move next.

His dark eyes narrowed as they met mine. "Fuck, yes. Don't want anyone touching these again. You understand? They're only for me."

He punctuated his last statement by twisting the silver barbell impaled through my left nipple. I moaned, arching my back as a wave of pleasure shot through me.

"Well, lucky for you that no one else but my piercing teacher has touched them." I swallowed hard, meeting his dark stare. "Nobody, ever."

He swallowed hard, his Adam's apple bobbing in his throat.

"No one?"

The time had come to admit my truth. I hoped that his possessiveness would extend to this, and he'd be happy I was untouched instead of scaring him away.

"I'm a virgin," I whispered, as though it was my dirty little secret.

His hands trailed down, cupping my already soaking pussy. "I'll be the first to taste this sweetness?"

"Uh-huh," I managed to breathe out, my body shivering under his touch. "You want to taste me?"

"Oh, baby, I want to do more than taste you. I want all of you." His hands rubbed between my thighs. "Do you want to feel my tongue on your pretty pussy?"

"Yes, please," I panted, already grinding against his palm.

"Love that my girl is needy for me," he murmured, gliding his fingers through my wetness.

Then as quickly as he started, he pulled his hand away, and I whimpered.

He smirked. "Don't worry, baby. I'm not gonna stop. It's just that the first time I make you come, it's gonna happen on my tongue."

I didn't even have time to react before he crawled

between my legs. I stared down at him as he smirked, his mouth hovering above my bare pussy, and all reasons to protest left my body.

He was gentle at first, placing the lightest kiss on my mound before he slowly slid his tongue across my slit. I wiggled in anticipation. No man had ever touched me there, and the way Fox looked at my pussy as though he was ready to devour it had me on the brink of exploding.

He pushed my thighs open so I was spread out like a feast, awaiting his watering mouth. Then he nuzzled my clit gently before sucking the sensitive bud in his mouth, and I involuntarily bucked my hips forward.

"Fox," I breathed hard.

"You're so sensitive, baby. I love that," he said, speaking the words right into my bare pussy.

He hooked a finger inside me, and I bucked forward, my legs shaking as he added another finger, pumping in and out of me. "You're so fucking tight. I need to get you loosened up to take my cock."

My breath hitched at his dirty words, then skittered out of me in a cry as his lips went back to my clit, lapping me up as he continued fucking me with his fingers. Instinctively, I met his rhythm, bucking my hips as I chased my orgasm.

He groaned into my clit, his eyes locking with mine. That dark stare was all I needed to fall over the edge, crying out as my body shook around his talented mouth.

He lapped up every last drop, taking in my after-shocks before he kissed a line up my stomach to hover over me, all tanned and tattooed flesh.

And his dick.

Holy hell, his beautiful dick that I desperately wanted to feel inside me.

There was more precome dripping off the edge. Reaching between us, I stroked my thumb along the tip, then rubbed the sticky liquid on my lips.

"Fuck, baby, that was so damn sexy. Do you like the way I taste?"

"Yes," I breathed, licking away the salty flavor.

A low growl came from deep within his throat before his lips were back on mine, his tongue devouring me as our naked bodies pressed together.

He wasn't even inside me but feeling the hard ridges of his massive dick rubbing against my my pussy lips had me grinding against him, chasing another orgasm.

He laughed, pulling back from our kiss. "You're my greedy girl, aren't you? Do you want my cock that bad? Want me to take this cherry? Because you gotta know, if you give it to me, there's no going back. You're mine. You want to be mine, baby?"

"Yes, please," I begged, reaching between us and fisting his shaft, barely able to get my fingers around it.

"Your hand feels damn good around me," he murmured, leaning back so he could position his head right against my slit. "But your tight pussy is gonna be even better."

I sucked in a deep breath as he stared at me with hooded eyes.

"Don't worry, baby," he soothed. "I'm gonna go slow. Tell me if it hurts, okay?"

"Uh-huh," I panted.

Slowly he inched in the head of his dick, muttering as he sat there, not moving. "Fuck you're so tight. I need you to spread those creamy thighs more for me so I can fill you with every inch of my cock."

My legs were already like jelly, but I spread them farther as he sank in deeper, filling me to the hilt in one quick thrust. A ripple of pleasure and pain ripped through me, and I let out a whimper.

"You okay, Dahlia? Because once I start, I'm not stopping until you come on my dick. Then I'm gonna keep going. Fill you up with my come until it's flowing down your pretty thighs."

"Yes, please," I breathed, gripping his shoulders and pulling his lips to mine.

At first, he rocked his body slowly, but I didn't want to slow and steady. So I kissed him harder, moving my hips against his, relishing in the delicious friction between our bodies.

So this was what the big deal was with sex.

Or maybe it was just with Fox because I couldn't imagine anyone else comparing to this.

"So close," I panted.

"Good because I need you to come for me before I fill you," he murmured into my neck as his hand slid between us.

His thumb was on my clit, circling it in the same rhythm his dick pumped in and out of me. My breath caught as I matched his movement, slamming my eyes shut as my toes curled and my entire body exploded. Then I screamed, unable to keep back my emotions as my whole body shook underneath him.

He grunted, pumping harder until his body stilled over me. My nails dug into his ass as his dick jerked inside me. Then he collapsed, breathing into my neck before leaving featherlight kisses in his wake. The endorphin rush—combined with all the adrenaline from earlier today—left me exhausted. So when Fox rolled on his back and settled me against his chest, my eyes drifted close, and I quickly fell asleep.

6

FOX

"That's it, baby," I grunted as I slammed into Dahlia's tight pussy over and over. "Squeeze my cock. Make me come so I'll stuff you full of my come."

Her legs rested on my shoulders, and I held her ass up so I could sink as deep as possible with every punch of my hips.

"Kye," she moaned, her hands fisting in the sheets as her head thrashed from side to side.

"Fucking love the way you say my name when I'm inside you," I groaned, pumping faster and harder. "So tight. Fuck!"

Dahlia tensed and whimpered, "I'm going to come."

"Do it, baby," I ordered. "Want your body ripe

and ready to take everything I give you." I'd done my best to fuck her bare as often as possible over the past three days, determined to plant my kid in her belly.

Her tits bounced from the force of my thrusts, and I used one hand to gently tug on the piercing on each nipple, making the muscles in her pussy spasm.

"Yessss. Oh! Oh, yes! Kye!"

She pressed her head back into the mattress, and her back arched as her orgasm crashed over her. The sound of her screaming my name in ecstasy disintegrated the last of my control, and I buried myself as deep as possible and roared as my cock exploded inside her. "Fuck, yes!"

Black spots floated in my vision, and I felt light-headed as bursts of come continually filled her. It seemed like I had an endless supply of spunk, filling her so full that it spilled out. Eventually, I finally appeared to be empty, and I collapsed on top of her, keeping my weight on my elbows so I wouldn't crush her. I let her legs fall to her sides but quickly stuffed a pillow under her hips to keep her elevated. I didn't want any more of my seed escaping.

Dahlia panted heavily, and I felt her racing heartbeat where our chests touched. My face was buried in her neck, but when she let out a cute little sigh, I lifted my head and gazed down at her. "Love watching you come, baby," I murmured.

"I think you've made that pretty clear by the number of orgasms you've given me," she teased.

I raised an eyebrow and rocked my hips forward. "Complaining?"

Her pussy clenched, and a shiver wracked her body, making me grin wickedly.

"Nooooo," she moaned, squeezing her eyes shut.

I wasn't sure if she was saying no to my question or climaxing again so soon. Probably both, but I chose to latch onto the latter. "Yes," I said firmly as my pace picked up. "Need another one, baby."

An hour later, Dahlia had practically passed out in post-orgasmic bliss. While I wanted nothing more than to curl myself around her and follow suit, some shit at home needed handling.

I'd been watching the weather, and though the storm had blown through after a couple of days, the bridge was still flooded. My morning had started with my mouth between my woman's legs and ended with her pussy wrapped around my cock, so I hadn't had a chance to check on anything in a while.

Quietly, I climbed out of bed and pulled on a pair of sweatpants, then padded out to the small kitchen table where I'd left the sat phone, my cell, and my laptop. Power had been restored yesterday, along with cell service, so I sent a quick text to Lex, asking about the road. A part of me hoped we were still stuck in this little bubble we'd created, but I had responsibilities I couldn't shirk.

As soon as our Wi-Fi connection had been restored, I'd checked on investments, answered pressing emails from the many people who managed the club's businesses, and any other urgent shit I could handle remotely.

My phone beeped, and I picked it up, frowning when I saw Lex's message letting me know the road was open. I fired off a text to Mav, giving him an ETA on when I'd be returning and asked if he'd heard anything from Mac.

I knew Deviant had laid a false trail, but that didn't stop me from being a little paranoid. Dahlia needed to be pregnant and hopelessly in love with me by the time we had a confrontation with her father.

His response came in fast, letting me know that we needed to talk about Cordell when I returned and that Mac had pestered Molly a little until he realized she really didn't know where Dahlia was.

Satisfied for the moment, I made a couple of omelets and was just sliding them onto plates when my girl wandered out of the bedroom looking sexy and adorably rumpled.

"Hey, baby," I greeted her as she sidled up next to me. Bending my head, I kissed her before smacking her ass. "I made breakfast. We need to eat and get on the road."

Disappointment flashed in her beautiful green eyes, and I smiled as I grasped her hips and lifted her to sit on the counter.

"If I had my way, we'd stay a while so I could fuck you uninterrupted around the clock. But I need to get back to my responsibilities."

"I understand." There wasn't a single spark of resentment or anything else negative in her expression. Warmth spread through my chest at yet another example of how perfectly Dahlia fit with me.

After setting our food on the table, I picked her up and carried her over, then sat in a chair and settled her on my lap. Over the past few days, when we weren't fucking, we spent time getting to know each other. So while we ate, I answered more questions about the club and my work. I also told her about the tattoo shop we owned, where Molly would be working, and mentioned we were considering hiring someone to do piercings. The part I didn't mention was that there was no way in hell I'd ever let her touch another man's junk...or even a woman's pussy or tits. I just hoped she'd be happy doing earlobes and shit instead.

Once we'd finished our meal and cleaned up, I carried her to the shower where I thoroughly dirtied her up, then washed her clean. Until she was carrying my baby, I didn't want to waste my come outside her womb, but I'd been powerless to deny her when she'd dropped to her knees and took me in her mouth. Fuck, she gave head like a porn star when she followed my directions like a good girl. My climax had made me weak in the knees.

Afterward, we packed up and left for Old Bridge. With the heavy rain the last time I'd had Dahlia on my bike, I hadn't been able to enjoy it. On the ride home, I noticed everything. The way her arms held tight around my waist, her tits pressed against my back, and her thick thighs cradling my hips. I was hard as steel during the entire trip, and when we finally drove onto the compound, I could barely think about anything except dragging Dahlia up to my room and fucking her brains out.

Unfortunately, Maverick waited for me when we walked into the clubhouse from the garage.

"Dahlia?" Molly gasped as she walked into the common room. "What are you doing here?"

"I can't leave you here to go through your pregnancy alone, now can I?"

Shit. Technically, I hadn't lied. I'd only insinuated that Molly was pregnant when I met Dahlia at the airport, but I wasn't sure how she would react to the distinction.

"Pregnancy?" Molly repeated at the same time Maverick growled, "She isn't alone."

I shot a warning glare at my VP, telling him without words to be careful how he spoke to my woman.

"I guess I could be..." Molly mused before anyone said anything else.

Dahlia frowned. "You don't know?" Then she eyed me suspiciously, but I just stared at her, letting her feel the heat from my gaze. Yeah, I wasn't the least bit sorry for what I'd done, not when it ended up with Dahlia beneath me.

She blushed and looked back at her sister. "Maybe you should go to the doctor and find out."

"We'll go see Blade, princess," Maverick interjected. "Just give me a few minutes to update Fox."

Knowing it was club business, Molly nodded. "I'll meet you there. He can do the test, but I'll wait for you to find out."

He snaked his arm around her waist and yanked

her body into his before kissing the hell out of her and leaving her in a dazed state. "I promise, princess, if you're not pregnant, I'm gonna fuck you day and night until the next test is positive." He winked, and pink stained her cheeks.

"Sounds like hard work. I hope you're up for the job."

Maverick laughed—something I'd rarely seen him do before he met Molly since he was almost as grumpy as me—and patted her ass as the girls walked away.

We walked to my office in silence, and he shut the door behind him when we entered. I dropped into the chair behind my desk and straightened the stack of files waiting for me on the left side, then flipped a pen in the holder so that they were all right side up. I shot Mav a dirty look, knowing he was the most likely culprit. The guys loved to move shit just to irritate me. "What's going on with the Cordell situation?"

Maverick leaned back in his seat and rested his ankle on the opposite knee. "Nic called to let us know that Cordell's been demoted and asked that we let him know if the little shit tries to contact us." Maverick's tone was harsh, and I wondered if the added irritation stemmed from an escalation of some kind.

"Has he?"

Mav nodded. "Tried to backpedal, but when he realized we weren't going to believe his bullshit, he started spouting shit, and I hung up. I had Deviant trace the call, but it was a burner. He's gone underground. So I sent Nic a text, and he said he'd take care of it."

Knowing Nic, Cordell was in for a world of pain. As the head of his family, he was not an unfair or overly harsh leader, but he kept his position by instilling respect and a healthy amount of fear into others. Nic didn't like to be disobeyed, and his methods of punishment were dark. Something we had in common.

I nodded. "He sent me a new order," I informed my VP. "Got a message from Brandon, too. Seems Carly wasn't happy with their last supply purchase, and he talked her into giving us a shot."

Brandon was Nic's cousin and had been his number two until Brandon married into the mob. Literally. His wife, Carly, was the head of the Irish mob in the Northeast.

I gave him a couple of orders, then watched him

rush out of the room, intent on finding his old lady. After a few minutes of trying to work, I gave up and went in search of my woman as well. Hopefully, we'd be visiting Blade for a pregnancy test soon, and I was determined for it to be positive, which meant I needed to get Dahlia back to our room so I could get back to working on it.

7

DAHLIA

W hile our men left to take care of club business, my sister led me out the back to a building directly behind the Iron Rogues clubhouse. The Iron Rogues had a clinic back there, which came in handy when you needed an unexpected pregnancy test. Although they probably needed it for more serious medical issues since it turned out to be fully decked out with an x-ray machine and all sorts of other equipment.

"I can't believe I didn't think about the possibility of being pregnant yet," Molly muttered, shaking her head while we waited for Blade, the Iron Rogues doctor, to join us.

I rolled my eyes with a sigh. "And I can't believe

that Fox tricked me into not getting on my flight by telling me you were expecting Maverick's baby."

"Okay, that explains what you said when you got here." Molly climbed onto the exam table and perched on the edge. "But not what's going on between you and the Iron Rogues prez. Where've you been for the past few days? And more importantly, what have you been up to?"

She wagged her brows to emphasize her last question, making me giggle. "Probably the same stuff you got up to with Maverick when he carried you out of Silver Ink and brought you here, only I have a hurricane to thank for stranding me in a place with only one bed."

"Holy crap," Molly shrieked, rubbing her hands together. "You and Fox are like a romance novel. You've got an MC president chasing a princess from another club. Plus an age gap, a hurricane, and the all-time favorite only one bed trope!"

I quirked a brow and planted a fist on my hip. "Like you can talk. You were literally tossed over Maverick's shoulder. He's the Iron Rogues VP, and you're a club princess just like me, and he had to shoot some guy stalking you. That's all book-worthy, too."

"Fair   point,"   she   conceded   with   a   grin.

"Although, one thing our stories don't have in common is that Dad has reluctantly given his blessing for my relationship. But he has no clue what you've been up to with Fox."

"Yet," I sighed, dropping onto one of the chairs with a sigh. "But I'm sure that'll only last for so long. Eventually, he'll realize I'm not in Europe and will start looking closer to home."

She gave me the side-eye. "Girl, you better come up with a better plan than that. I had you covering for me at home, but you don't have the same advantage. Dad noticed your car was here and then gone when everything went down with Fritz, and Maverick pointed out to him that Fox was missing too."

"Dammit," I hissed, raking my fingers through my hair. "I hope he's not keeping close tabs on Fox. I want more time with him before we have to deal with Dad, but if someone reported to him that I just rode into the compound on the back of Fox's bike, we both know what'll happen."

She nodded with a grimace. "Yeah, he'd be here in no time flat."

"And then I'd have to throw you under the bus to get out of trouble with him," I teased.

Molly narrowed her eyes at me. "How would you

do that?"

"By telling him that you're preggers." I grinned at her. "Then he can lose his shit over his baby girl having a baby."

"But we don't even know if that's true," she protested, shaking her head. "I haven't taken a test yet."

"That's where I come in," Blade muttered as he strode into the clinic. "It's a good thing I know how determined Mav is to knock you up, or else I would've had to send one of the prospects out for a urine test. Never needed one before now. Gonna have to keep them stocked up now that my club brothers are falling like flies. If I wasn't a doctor, I'd have to worry about it being contagious."

"I don't know," I drawled, beaming a mischievous smile at him. "From the stories I've heard growing up, it certainly seems as though the happily ever afters spread through the Silver Saints clubhouse after my dad fell for my mom."

"Too true," Molly agreed. "And their relationship started with a kidnapping like mine did with Maverick."

"Plus, you have two Mackenzies here now," I added. "That would only make it spread even faster, right?"

Heaving a deep sigh, Blade shook his head as he decided to ignore our teasing and focus on the reason we were in his clinic. "You want to pee on a stick or have me draw your blood?"

"Which one is faster?" Molly asked.

"You'll get the results from the urine test in a few minutes, but I'll want to confirm with a blood test if it comes back positive. That has to get sent out to the lab, but I can have a prospect run it over right away, so we'd know in a day or two," he explained.

"Okay, I'll pee on a stick for now, but I want to wait until Maverick's here to see the results."

My sister's answer made me smile. "Aw, that's so sweet."

Blade yanked a box out of a drawer and ripped it open before thrusting a stick at Molly. "Go piss on this."

She slid off the exam table and padded over to the bathroom across from us. Blade chuckled when I followed her, but we were sisters who were only a year apart in age, so we had peed in front of each other tons of times.

"Crap, this is harder than I expected," she grumbled. "Aiming while peeing just isn't something girls learn how to do."

I wrinkled my nose. "Remind me to just jump to

the blood test when it's my turn."

She got up and set the test facedown before washing her hands, grinning at me through the mirror. "It would be so amazing if we were pregnant at the same time. Our kids could grow up as two peas in a pod just like we did!"

"Only if they don't get up to the same things we did as teenagers." I shook my head with a laugh, remembering some of our antics.

Molly shrugged. "If Dad wasn't so strict with us, maybe we wouldn't have tried to break the rules so often."

"Which makes it super ironic that we both fell for guys with that same overprotective streak," I pointed out.

"Crap, you're right," she groaned as we left the bathroom.

Watching my big sister take a pregnancy test and talking about the possibility of us having kids at the same time made me think about all of the times Fox and I had sex without any protection. Although we hadn't really talked about it other than during the heat of the moment, I knew the risk I was taking. So when Blade looked up from his phone, I asked, "How early can someone take a test?"

Blade's focus shifted to me. "Blood tests can tell

if you're pregnant ten days after conception. Any sooner, and you run the risk of a false negative."

"By someone, do you mean you?" Molly squealed, bouncing on the exam table.

My cheeks filled with heat. "Yeah...um...I do, but it's too early to tell since it hasn't been a week yet."

"Well, shit," Blade sighed. "I guess I'll need to stock up on those damn tests more than I thought if it's possible that the prez has already knocked you up."

"If Fox is anything like Mav, then that's absolutely the right call," Molly agreed with a grin. "My man is obsessed with knocking me up. Just last night—"

"I don't need to hear this shit about my club brothers," Blade muttered as he headed toward the door.

"Just wait until you find your old lady," Molly teased with a laugh. "And if it's soon, then maybe you'll rethink the whole contagious thing, even if it's scientifically impossible."

He paused to glare at her over his shoulder and growled, "Not gonna happen."

We were giggling at his vehement denial when Maverick raced past him and asked, "Is it over? How did everything go?"

"Good." Molly beamed a smile at him. "All I had to do was pee on a stick after giving Blade a hard time about finding a woman of his own so he'd be as deliriously happy as we are."

"How soon will we know?"

Molly jerked her chin toward the bathroom. "The results are probably ready now, but I promised you I'd wait to look, so I left it in there."

As I watched Maverick tug her inside to see if she was pregnant, Fox came up behind me and wrapped his arms around my front. "C'mon, baby. Let's give them some privacy."

As curious as I was to know if the test was positive, I knew this was a special moment for them as a couple. "Yeah."

Fox led me back to the clubhouse, and when we reached the back door, I heard Maverick yell, "I'm gonna be a dad!"

"Woohoo! I'm gonna be an aunt," I hollered back.

Fox nudged me into the building. "How about we go up to our room so I can make sure you'll be a mommy soon too, if I haven't already gotten the job done."

Butterflies swirled in my belly. "Yes, please."

8

FOX

"Need you naked now," I growled as I stalked into our bedroom on the upper floor of the clubhouse. This level was filled with rooms, some permanently occupied by brothers, and others for those who needed to crash from time to time. Maverick and I had the largest suites on opposite ends of the building.

I hurried through the living area and into the bedroom, then set Dahlia on her feet next to the bed.

"Strip," I ordered her as I went to work on my own clothing. I shrugged out of my cut and practically ripped my black T-shirt over my head but stopped there to watch my woman. With every bared inch of her silky, sweet skin, my mouth watered, and the fire building inside me became a raging inferno.

When she was finally naked, I bent down and picked up my cut from where it had fallen on the floor.

I held it out and waited. She hesitated at first, making me scowl, but then she turned and slipped her arms through the holes. I rested the vest on her shoulders before turning her back to face me. "Fucking hell, baby. Been dreaming about seeing you wearing my my cut and nothin' else. Only thing that would make it better was if it was my property patch on your back."

Dahlia's eyes widened, and I smirked. "Weren't you listening, baby? I told you when you let me inside you and gave me that sweet cherry that there was no going back."

Crimson bloomed on her cheekbones, and her lips curled up into a smile. "I thought maybe it was just the heat of the moment. I didn't want to assume..."

I rolled my eyes and grabbed both sides of the cut, using it to drag her body up against me. "You really think I'd have spent all this time fucking you bare if I didn't intend to make you mine?"

A pretty blush stole across her cheeks, and she shook her head.

"Now that we've cleared that shit up, I'm gonna fuck you while you're branded with my name." The thought grew, and I made a mental note to talk to her about having Molly give her a permanent brand. The property patch was for others, so everyone would know she'd been claimed and to keep their fucking hands and eyes to themselves. But having my name inked on her creamy skin...that would be just for us.

I grasped her waist and lifted her up, then put her in the center of the bed. Then I stood at the end and drank in the mouthwatering sight of my woman laid out bare for me. "Show me that pussy that belongs to me, baby," I demanded.

Slowly, Dahlia spread her legs, giving me a perfect view of her naked, drenched center. *Fuck.* My cock leaked, and the sensitive head rubbed painfully against my jeans.

Keeping my eyes on her, I quickly removed the rest of my clothes, then climbed onto the bed. I got down onto my stomach, wedging my shoulders between her thighs, and slipped my hands under her sexy ass. "You smell so fucking amazing."

She tasted even better. Taking my time and enjoying every sip, I lapped at her pussy and swallowed her juices. When she tried to raise her hips, I gently slapped her pussy before slipping my hand beneath her butt cheek again. "Stay still," I growled. "Or I'll stop."

"Please," she begged, tunneling her hands into my hair and pulling desperately.

"Not going to rush me, Dahlia. Just relax."

"Relax?" she huffed. "You're the one making me needy, so you should take care of it!"

I grinned. "Oh, I will, baby. But I'm gonna do it my way."

Ignoring her cute little growl, I went back to my snack. The sounds she made drove me crazy, made me desperate to hear her falling apart around my dick. But I kept myself in check and lazily explored what belonged to me. Eventually, I pushed two fingers into her channel and curled them upward as I blew lightly on her clit.

Dahlia moaned and squirmed. "Kye..." Her hips bucked, and I pulled back, giving her thigh a smack and glaring at her.

"Last warning, Dahlia."

She nodded and bit her lip so hard the skin turned white.

Using my lips, tongue, teeth, and fingers, I slowly tortured her, building her up and easing her back down. I knew the pressure inside her was growing, and when I finally let her come, it would be *hard*. I was determined to make sure she remembered everything about the first time I fucked her while she was in our bed, wearing my cut.

Knowing how loud she was when she climaxed and how much of a frenzy I was working her up to, I made the decision to start looking for another place to live in the morning. For now, I needed to make sure no one else heard her cries of pleasure because I would kill anyone who saw or heard what was meant for only me.

When she was trembling with pent-up desire, and her skin was flushed from her face to the tips of her toes, I zeroed in on her hard little nub. I sucked it into my mouth just as my fingers scraped over her most sensitive inner spot. Then I slid one of my hands out from under her and clamped it over her mouth just in time to muffle her scream as she splintered apart. The sound went straight to my dick, and I ground my pelvis into the mattress to try to hold off my release.

When she began to descend from her high, I placed a soft kiss on her pubic bone and got to my knees.

"Holy cow," she muttered, her choppy breaths making her tits bounce, the piercings twinkling in the light. "That was..."

I grinned wickedly.

"That was...mean."

My head fell back as laughter burst from my chest. "Maybe," I conceded when my chuckles faded. "But I bet you'd let me do it again any time I want."

Dahlia pressed her lips together and narrowed her eyes, but after a beat, she blew out a breath and muttered, "Yeah."

Fuck, she was cute. And sexy as hell. And damn near perfect.

I placed my palms on her calves and glided them up her legs and stomach to span her rib cage, stopping when my thumbs were at the underside of her breasts. My cut had fallen open, putting her big tits on display. I licked my lips before bending low and wrapping them around one of the taut buds, using my tongue to flick the little barbell attached to it. I cupped both globes, holding them firmly while I played. "Fucking love these," I grunted as I switched to the opposite breast.

"Kye," Dahlia said, her tone pleading as she arched her back, pressing the mound deeper into my mouth. "I need you in me."

"You beg so pretty, baby," I crooned before placing a kiss on each peak. "I want to hear more, but if I don't get inside you soon, I'm gonna lose my mind."

"Yes. Inside me, now." I pulled back, scowling at her demanding tone.

"Who do you belong to, Dahlia?"

"You," she sighed, frustration coloring her tone.

"Fucking right. And that means I'm in charge. Gonna take this pussy any way I want, when I want, understood?"

Her piercing green orbs flashed with raw desire, and I swallowed a grin. I'd quickly learned that my baby liked it when I took control. "Yes," she whispered.

"Good girl."

I guided her legs up to wrap around my waist and moved into position, notching the tip of my dick in her opening. "Fucking soaked," I rasped as her juices coated the fat head of my cock. Come spurted out, mixing our essences, and it snapped my remaining control. Punching my fists into the mattress for leverage, I slammed home, burying myself balls deep inside her. "Fuck!" I shouted as her pussy clamped tight around my pulsing shaft. I was a big guy with a long, thick cock, but despite our size difference, Dahlia took me like she was made for me.

Her walls were snug as hell, and it made it difficult to last, especially when they rippled with pleasure.

"Mouth," I demanded as I began to move inside her. She raised her head, and I captured her lips in a hungry, soul-deep kiss. Her pussy was snug, and I had to drag my dick out before shoving it back in. I broke away from her mouth so we could catch our breath.

"Harder, Kye," Dahlia moaned. "Please."

"You want me to fuck you, baby?" I growled as I dragged my dick along her walls.

"Yes! Fuck me!"

I reached above her and grasped the headboard for support before thrusting hard and deep.

"Yes!" she cried.

My hips pistoned back and forth, gaining speed until I was rutting between her thighs, taking her with primal instincts, intent on branding her inside and out.

"Fuck, baby," I muttered. "Could live in this pussy. Oh, fuck yeah. Squeeze me, baby. Fuck! Oh fuck!"

"Yes! Oh, Kye! Yes!"

Dahlia clung to my torso, but as she neared her climax, she cupped her tits, and I groaned, "Yeah, baby. Play with those tits. Fuck!"

She plucked her nipples, then rubbed her tits against my chest so that the piercings scraped over my skin. Her channel gripped me like a vise, and her eyes rolled back in her head. I knew she was about to come, so I leaned down and covered her mouth with my own.

Her body went taut, then she broke apart as I swallowed her screams of ecstasy.

The feel of her climax rippling in her pussy pushed me over the edge. I threw back my head and roared as my orgasm barreled into me with the force of a fucking freight train.

When I was empty and the adrenaline began to ebb, I rolled to my side, taking Dahlia with me so she was sprawled over my body. I kissed her bare shoulder before burying my face in her red curls.

I was fucking addicted to this woman. And there wasn't anything I wouldn't do to keep her.

9

DAHLIA

Waking up with Fox's arms wrapped around me was one of my favorite perks of being with him. Behind the orgasms, of course.

I loved the quiet moments in the morning when there weren't any distractions. Just the two of us and the start of a new day. "You know what I just realized?"

"What, baby?" he asked, brushing a kiss against my neck.

"I was never a morning person until you." I turned in his embrace to smile up at him. "I used to need a couple of cups of coffee before I was ready to face the world or else I'd be all grumpy and shit."

He cupped my cheeks with his large, calloused palms. "I can't picture you being grouchy as fuck, but

I kinda want to see it. I bet you're gorgeous as hell with a frown on your beautiful face and your pretty green eyes sleepy."

Butterflies swirled in my belly at his compliment. "Aw, that's sweet, but trust me when I say you don't want to meet cranky Dahlia. She's no fun at all."

"We're gonna have to agree to disagree, baby." He claimed my mouth in a deep kiss that left me breathless. "And don't feel like you need to hide it from me if you're in a funk. I want to see every side of you because you're all mine. From head to toe, no matter your mood."

"If you keep saying sweet things like that, you'll never have to worry about me being grumpy again. I'll be too busy swooning."

"I'll keep that in mind, baby. But just know that you can have the best of both worlds if you want. Your morning cuddle with me and coffee since I can get a prospect to bring up a cup each morning," he offered.

I shook my head. "Forget caffeine. I probably should've realized long ago that all I needed was a daily injection of the big D instead."

"Not until you met me," he growled, rolling me onto my back and pressing his body against mine. "I wasn't joking about every fucking inch of you being mine, Dahlia. I'm the only one who gives you the orgasms you love so much."

The mind-blowing releases he gave me weren't the only thing I loved, but I hadn't gotten up the courage to say that particular four-letter word to him yet. It was only a matter of time, though, because my feelings kept growing each day we spent together.

Stroking my palms up his chest, I nodded. "I know I'm all yours, Kye. You're the only man I've ever really seen. The only one I've wanted."

"Damn fucking straight."

He kissed me again until I writhed beneath him, ready for another dose of his big D even though he'd taken me a couple of times in the middle of the night already. Including just a few hours ago. But my libido didn't seem to have an off switch since I met Fox, so when there was a knock on the door, I whimpered in protest. "No."

"Don't worry, baby. This isn't about club business or anything that's gonna pull me away from you," he reassured me as he slid off the mattress, tugged on a pair of jeans, and strode out the bedroom door.

Sitting up, I lifted the sheet to cover my chest and leaned over to see if I could see what was happening at the front door. When I couldn't get a good view, I scooted off the bed and wrapped the sheet around me to peek into the living room.

Fox must have heard me because he angled his body so I couldn't see anything after he opened the door, which made me curious.

"Here you go, Prez."

Fox took a brown paper bag from him and said, "Thanks, Tank."

"Sorry it wasn't ready sooner," Tank apologized.

"Didn't expect your old lady to be a miracle worker. She did it plenty fast. Give her my gratitude for making this a priority."

"Course she did. It isn't every day that the prez—"

Fox didn't let him finish. "She's awake and doesn't know what this is about yet."

"Shit, sorry. I'll leave you to it, then. Congratulations, man."

Fox jerked his chin up in acknowledgment before shutting the door.

"What's with all the secrecy if it isn't about club business?" I asked, crossing my arms over my chest to hold the sheet in place.

"A surprise you're gonna love." There was a possessive gleam in his eyes as he stalked back into the bedroom that sent a sensual shiver down my spine since it was the same way he looked when his dick was deep inside me.

I climbed back on the bed, and he sat beside me. "How can you be so sure?"

He tugged the sheet until it pooled at my waist and tugged on one of my nipple piercings. "We might not have been together long, but I know you, baby. Inside and out. And you want this as much as I do."

"When you put it like that, I really need to know what the surprise is."

"Good thing I wasn't planning to make you wait, then." He reached into the bag and pulled out a leather vest. One that was much smaller than his.

My breath caught in my throat as I realized exactly what he held. "Yeah, you had every reason to be sure I would love this."

"Of course, I did." He unfolded the vest so I could see the property patch on the back that proclaimed me to be his. Then he slid my arms through the holes and leaned back to take in how I looked wearing it. "Because you were born to be mine."

"I really was," I agreed with a sniffle.

"No crying, baby."

I beamed him a watery smile. "I'm just so happy we found each other."

He kissed away my tears before claiming my mouth. Just as things started to get hot and heavy between us, there was another knock on the door. I whimpered in protest again. "Seriously? Why does everyone have the worst timing ever today? I'm going to end up with the female version of blue balls if people keep coming up here like this."

"Quit complaining and get out here," Molly called. "I want to see your property vest, and we were supposed to go shopping today, remember?"

"How in the hell does she already know about this?" I asked, pointing at the leather vest he'd just given me.

Fox shook his head with a chuckle. "You know how fast gossip spreads in a clubhouse."

"Too true." I sighed.

"Shopping?" he asked.

"Yeah, my sister planned to show me her favorite places in Old Bridge today." I tugged on one of the loops at the waist of his jeans. "I meant to mention it last night, but then you distracted me with all of your sexiness."

"Which he better not do again right now," Molly yelled through the door.

"Go away," I called back.

"Nope. I'm pregnant, hungry, and the only thing I want is a big stack of cinnamon apple French toast from the diner downtown. Let's go," she demanded.

"Geesh," I sighed as I crawled off the mattress. "Give me a minute to get dressed."

"I'll give you five, but that's all."

I widened my eyes at Fox as she stomped away loudly enough that I could hear her footsteps through the closed door. "You still sure I'd be cute even when I'm a giant grouch? Because I sound an awful lot like my sister did just then."

He nodded. "Looking forward to seeing it when you're having your own pregnancy cravings, baby."

With how often we were having unprotected sex, that would probably be sooner rather than later. "Then I guess I'd better go see if that French toast is as good as Molly thinks."

"It's fucking fantastic." He went into the closet and grabbed a shirt while I dressed. "Which is why I'm joining you two."

It ended up being the four of us since Maverick didn't want to let Molly out of his sight. But we decided to take two vehicles, just in case something came up and one of the guys had to leave before we were done shopping. Which turned out to be the right call, but for a completely different reason.

"It's a damn good thing we brought your truck, too," Maverick muttered a few hours later. "Had no clue my woman could shop like this."

Molly narrowed her eyes at him as she shoved three more bags against his chest. "Are you really complaining about your pregnant woman buying new clothes and a few things for the baby?"

"Absolutely not, princess." Gathering the bags in one hand, he reached out to tug her close with the other. "If you want to buy out the whole fucking store, I'll call every damn prospect and tell them to get their asses down here so they can take everything back to the clubhouse for you."

Grinning up at Fox, I jerked my chin toward his club brother. "That was the perfect answer. You should take notes."

"Don't need to." He brushed a quick kiss against my lips. "I know exactly how to handle you, baby."

"True." I winked at him. "And when my sister is finally done shopping, you can handle me all you want. In bed. And we better not be interrupted again."

"Fine, I'm done," Molly huffed. "You guys can load up this stuff, and then we can head back to the compound. But only because I'm in favor of your plan to knock up my sister so we can have our first babies together."

More than ready to leave, I beamed a smile at Fox. "I'll meet you at your truck."

While they headed toward Maverick's vehicle to put Molly's bags in the back, I crossed the parking lot toward Fox's extended cab. I was about ten feet away when the horn beeped to let me know he'd unlocked it for me. Then there was a loud boom, and everything went black.

"What the fuck happened?" I roared as I yanked at my hair, pacing in front of Dahlia's hospital room. "How did a bomb get in my damn truck? Someone is gonna die for hurting my woman."

The explosion had come out of fucking nowhere, and the blast had knocked us both off our feet. I'd scrambled over to Dahlia, only to find her unconscious. She'd been struck in the head by a flying piece of debris. Luckily, Maverick and Molly had been far enough away not to be impacted by the explosion.

I kept it together while we waited for the ambulance, and during the ride to the hospital and through the tests, where they finally determined that she only had a slight concussion and no other injuries.

Then I lost my shit.

"Deviant is on it, Fox," Whiskey grunted. He'd stepped in to handle things since Maverick was busy making sure Molly didn't go apeshit or have a meltdown. She'd been going back and forth between crying and demanding to know who to murder.

"I called Wraith, and he's looking over the device to see if he can find any hints as to who made it or at least where they got the parts."

Wraith had been serving in the Air Force when he patched, working as an EOD (Explosive Ordnance Disposal) tech. He'd retired a few years ago and now owned a security company.

"The second you know something," I snarled at Whiskey before storming back into Dahlia's room. She looked paler than usual, making her sexy freckles stand out in stark contrast against her creamy skin. There was a bandage on her left temple, and just the sight of it had anger bubbling inside me again. But I shoved my fury aside and shuffled over to sit beside her on the bed.

A little while later, Dahlia's eyes fluttered, and she whimpered, "Kye?"

"I'm here, baby."

She looked up at me, her expression frightened and confused. "What happened?"

"A bomb was planted in my truck. It went off when I unlocked it with the remote." I recapped what the doctors had said, trying to sound calm while I was a raging ball of fury on the inside. "They want to keep you overnight for observation" —I held up my hand when she opened her mouth, ostensibly to argue with me—"but Blade will handle it. We'll take you home, and he can monitor you there."

What I didn't tell her was that I wouldn't be able to breathe until she was safely locked in the compound. Especially since I needed to know that she would be protected because the second we located the motherfucker who'd hurt her, I was gonna put them in the ground.

It took a couple of hours to get the discharge straightened out, then Jake pulled up in one of the club's big, seven-seater, armored SUVs. We'd occasionally needed them for a run—depending on the item being transported and where it was being delivered.

Whiskey took shotgun while Mav and Molly climbed into the back, then Blade, Dahlia, and I took the middle row. I held her hand with my fingers resting over her pulse—the steady beat was the only thing keeping me calm.

When we arrived at the compound, I carried Dahlia to our room and tried to shut everyone out. However, Molly shoved her way past me, and I gritted my teeth while giving her exactly ten minutes to fuss over her sister.

"Okay, princess," Maverick said, walking toward his old lady while eyeing me like I was a ticking time bomb—no pun intended. "Dahlia needs to rest and spend some alone time with her man." Molly sputtered in protest, but Mav hurried her from the room.

Before I could do anything, there was a knock on the door.

"It's Blade. Brought pain meds for your girl."

"Hang tight, baby," I told Dahlia before stalking out of the bedroom and across the living room to open the door.

I stepped back to let Blade enter, then quickly shut the door before anyone took it as an invitation to visit.

"I'm gonna give her a shot for her pain," Blade explained as we moved toward the bedroom. "You can give her one of these pills every six hours if needed."

I took the bag he handed me and set it on the

dresser, my body filled with dread as I asked, "What if she's pregnant? They said at the hospital that it was too soon to tell, even with a blood test."

"It's safe for her to take," he confirmed. "Wasn't gonna give your woman anything that could do harm to a baby when I know you've been trying to knock her up."

"Thanks, man."

"Dahlia," Blade said softly as he padded over to her.

She blinked and struggled to sit up when she spotted my brother.

"Don't sit up," he urged before I could make the demand myself. "I need to check your vitals, then I'll give you meds and let you rest."

My phone vibrated in my pocket, and I pulled it out to see a text from Deviant. He had information, and while I knew I should step out since it was club business, I couldn't bring myself to leave Dahlia alone with Blade even though I trusted my club brother completely.

I walked to a corner by a window and called Deviant. "What did you find?"

"I'm sending you a picture. Let me know if you can ID the guy."

When the message came through, I was

surprised my phone didn't crack from my crushing grip. I didn't recognize the man in the photo, but it was apparent he was planting the bomb in my truck.

"Who the fuck is it?" I snarled.

"Some lowlife from a drug gang in Nashville. I already sent a couple of prospects out to grab him."

"You didn't think to run that by me first?" I was shocked that Deviant went around me and sent someone else to do my job. Dahlia was mine, which meant it was my right to track down the person who hurt her and make him suffer.

"He isn't the one you want to hunt, Prez. It's the man who paid for the materials and transferred five grand into the lackey's bank account who you're really gonna want to take down."

I had to admit, he'd made the right call. I couldn't go after both culprits, and he knew I'd want the mastermind. "Who?"

"Cordell DeLuca."

My jaw clenched so hard that my teeth ground together. I inhaled slowly, trying to hold myself together. I was known for being calm and cool under pressure, rarely lost my temper, and could be relied on for being rational. But when it came to my woman, all bets were off. The need to wrap my hands around Cordell's throat and watch the life drain from his eyes, was the only thing keeping me from losing my shit right that moment. I needed to keep my head in the game so I could hunt that asshole down.

And before I did, there was a call I needed to make.

I gave Deviant instructions on what to do next, then walked over to check on Dahlia. She wasn't moving, and for a second, fear clogged my throat.

"The meds will knock her out until tomorrow," Blade informed me when he saw my panicked expression.

Meds. Right. She wasn't unconscious again, just sleeping. Fuck. I needed to handle this shit before I did something stupid.

"I'll come by again in the morning."

I nodded and walked him to the door but stopped him before he left. "I'm riding out tonight. Going after the motherfucker who hurt Dahlia. Make sure someone takes over for you when I get back. Gonna need you to keep the asshole alive so I can make him pay...a lot."

Blade lifted his chin in acknowledgment. He didn't ask if I wanted him to come with me because he knew I'd want him here in case there was a complication with Dahlia's injuries.

After he left, I paced the living room as I put in a call to New York.

"DeLuca," Nic answered curtly.

"I need a favor," I said in lieu of a greeting.

"Most people start a phone call with hello, Kye," he replied dryly.

"Not when they are contemplating cold-blooded murder."

Nic was silent for a moment, then I heard rustling and the snick of a door closing.

"What's going on?"

"I'm calling for your help to find someone. And because we've been friends for so long and I respect you, I'm asking you to let me handle the situation rather than handing it over to you."

"Why would you need my permission?"

"Because I'm gonna kill someone in your family."

Nic sighed. "Cordell?"

"Who else?" I snarled.

"I told Maverick I would handle it. And I am. I located him this morning—"

"He almost killed my woman, Nic," I uttered in a ragged tone. Then I gave him a summary of what had happened with the bomb.

The Mafia boss went silent again. When he eventually spoke, his tone was lethal and hard as steel. "Women and children are off-limits. Cordell is no longer family. Handle him as you see fit."

"You said you knew where he is?"

"I'll do you one better. Stay by the phone. Next time I call, a package will be awaiting pick up somewhere near you."

"Are you sure? I'm willing to come to New York and hunt the asshole down."

"Unnecessary. It's your right to punish him, but it was me who brought the bastard into your life. Let me help. I wouldn't want to be that far away from my Gianna if it were me."

"I owe you," I replied. It was my way of saying thank you.

"I don't see it that way, but you're welcome."

I hung up and padded back into the bedroom. After setting my phone on the nightstand, I stripped down to my boxer briefs and climbed onto the bed. Curling myself around Dahlia, I reminded myself that she was okay and waited for Nic's call.

Motorcycle clubs were not the place to find men with clean hands. Some of us, like the Iron Rogues or Silver Saints, had honor, loyalty, and limits, but we were still involved in shady shit, had blood on our hands, and doled out our own brand of justice. At times, we'd worked with local law enforcement, but I was the judge and jury at moments like this. And in this case, I would also be the executioner.

I rode my bike out to a small building that sat at a spot on our property that was the farthest from any of the businesses, homes, and clubhouse. From the outside, it looked a lot like the safehouse Dahlia and I had holed up in. But on the inside, it was very, very different. We called it "The Room," a name as dismissive as its exterior. The interior had four rooms, a lounging area of sorts, a cell, an interrogation hold, and a space with a cache of...tools that might be needed to aid us in gaining what we wanted.

After parking my hog near the single entrance, I checked my phone again, re-reading Molly's text that assured me Dahlia was fine. I'd hated to leave my girl, but I needed to get this done so we could move on with our lives. Mav and Molly were watching over her, and that had to be enough for the moment.

The door of "The Room" opened, and Storm—the Iron Rogues Captain and an expert interrogator and negotiator—stepped out into the light of dawn.

"What kind of shape is he in?" I asked as I tucked my cell in my pocket and closed the distance between us. Nic had assured me that he would leave Cordell in one piece and "relatively healthy."

Storm grinned. "Couple of broken fingers, missing pinky, and a broken kneecap."

I couldn't help chuckling. *How very mafia.*

When I stepped inside, Blade was exiting the cell. He glanced up and nodded in greeting. "I bandaged the missing digit and set the broken ones in a splint. Kneecap is shattered though, not much I can do there."

"Bet he fell all over himself thanking you," Storm drawled, clearly relishing what came next. He could be a little bloodthirsty. But only when it came to fuckers who deserved it.

Cordell didn't know where he was or why he'd been brought here. So when Blade went in to fix him up, I could see how he might have been mislabeled as a hero.

"Put him in the blue room," I ordered as I walked through the third door on the right. I flipped on the light and glanced over my options. After some deliberation, I decided to go old school, grabbing a bat, brass knuckles, and a switchblade.

My gun was already loaded for the finale.

When I stepped into the room where Cordell was tied to a chair in the center, he looked at me with surprise, then his expression morphed into loathing and a hint of smug defiance.

"Looking awfully calm for someone who pissed off an Iron Rogue," Blade drawled as he leaned back against the wall.

"You wouldn't risk Nic's business by hurting his family," Cordell spat.

"Don't see any of his family here," I stated in a steely tone.

"Call Nic," he muttered, looking just a touch less confident.

"Who do you think gave me your location so fast?"

Cordell blanched. "He wouldn't betray family..."

"You might have gone after me, but my woman was caught in the crossfire. I don't know if you didn't think about that or didn't care, but either way, you crossed a big fucking line. Nic doesn't tolerate attacks against wives and children. You were already on thin ice with him. When he found out about my old lady, he washed his hands of you."

Cordell shrank into himself as the truth of his situation hit him. "I didn't mean for her to get hurt," he whined like a little bitch.

His eyes darted to the left, indicating he was lying, which added to my rage.

Stepping close, I rammed my fist into his jaw so hard it snapped his head back and rocked the chair. "You mean you didn't give a fuck if anyone else was hurt when you tried to kill me," I growled. "Lying to me isn't the smart play here."

"The truth won't save me."

"No," I agreed as I slipped on the brass knuckles. "You're gonna die for hurting my woman, but honesty might save you a little pain."

"Fine. I knew she'd probably be with you, but I figured if you were dead, you wouldn't care that she'd been killed too."

My next hit broke his nose, sending blood spurting out.

"I lied," I told him as I slipped into a side of me that felt little to no emotion, making me a deadly foe. "This is gonna hurt."

"DAMN, PREZ," Storm said with a low whistle. "And they call *me* bloodthirsty."

I rolled my eyes as I strode to a little kitchenette and started washing the blood off my hands.

"Brutal," Blade agreed. "Gotta say, though, Dahlia is your weakness now. You're always gonna have to be on your guard for people who'll try to get to you through her."

"You think I haven't already considered that? Dahlia deserves a fuck of a lot more than a man like me, but I'm just enough of a bastard not to care."

"Don't think I could give up my control like that," Storm mused as he cleaned the instruments I'd used to inflict hours of pain on the man who'd almost taken away the person who mattered most to me.

"When the right woman comes along, you won't care," I stated.

Blade scoffed. "Bullshit. The last thing I need is an old lady to deal with."

Storm muttered an agreement, and I just shook my head at their stupidity. It was almost funny that they thought they'd have a choice in the matter. I certainly hadn't. The second I saw Dahlia, I'd known there wasn't anything I wouldn't do to have her. She owned me from that moment on.

"Dispose of the body," I instructed as I dried my hands. "I need to get back to Dahlia." There was some other blood spatter on me, but I'd wanted to at least have clean hands for the ride home.

"Got it," Storm murmured.

I gave them a sharp lift of my chin in farewell, then walked out while they started talking about an upcoming car race that one of our enforcers—aptly named Racer—was driving in.

Once I arrived back at the clubhouse, I went to my office, where I had an extra change of clothes and used the attached bathroom to take a quick shower.

Before I could leave to head upstairs, a couple of prospects stopped in to report on an issue I'd had them taking care of. I schooled my patience and listened to their update, then walked swiftly toward the stairs. At least two other people stopped me, and as their president, I told myself I couldn't blow them off. However, when I shook off the last one, I dashed up the stairs and down the hall to my room.

Since I wasn't sure if Dahlia was awake yet, I entered as quietly as possible. Maverick was stretched out on the couch with a sleeping Molly curled into his side.

He lifted his chin in greeting and darted his eyes toward the bedroom before mouthing, "Asleep."

I nodded and silently entered the bedroom, then shut the door behind me. The blinds were closed, but it was late morning, so the room was still somewhat illuminated. Dahlia was on my side of the bed, curled around my pillow, her chest rising and falling in a slow, steady rhythm.

Without taking my eyes off her, I shed my clothing and climbed onto the mattress. Dahlia stirred as I pulled her into my arms and glanced down to see her sleepily blinking up at me.

"You got him?" she asked softly.

"Yeah, baby. He won't be a problem anymore."

She knew I wouldn't say anything else, and I waited for her to show some amount of annoyance over it. But she just smiled sweetly and snuggled deeper into my embrace.

I fucking loved everything about this woman, and when she healed, I was gonna drag her ass to the nearest courthouse and make her mine in every way.

The only question I wasn't sure how to answer was whether to talk to her father about us before or after she wore my ring. If I thought I could drag it out until I knew if she was pregnant, I'd definitely choose after. Because a marriage couldn't be annulled if the couple was expecting a baby.

However, I'd never been a coward, and I wasn't about to start now. And if my daughter had been injured by a car bomb, I'd want to know about it. So I owed him a call.

Maverick had already done the heavy lifting for us anyway. Mac had been forced to swallow having an Iron Rogue for a son-in-law, so why not two?

12

DAHLIA

It wasn't that long ago when I'd hoped my dad wouldn't find out about Fox and me because I wanted more time as a couple before he tried to interfere. But after everything that had happened in the past twenty-four hours, I raced across the clubhouse and threw myself at him when he showed up without letting us know he was coming.

"Dahlia, fuck." He wrapped his arms around me and pressed a kiss to the top of my head. "I came as soon as I heard. Are you okay?"

"Yeah, my head still hurts a little." I leaned back to peer up at him. "How did you find out?"

"I called him this morning."

I turned to gape at Fox. "You did?"

"Yeah," he confirmed with a nod. "Keeping him

out of the loop about our relationship was one thing. Hiding what happened with the car bomb was completely different. He's your dad. He deserved to know that you were hurt."

"Relationship?" Dad growled.

"How come you didn't tell me?"

Fox moved close enough to tug me against his side, ignoring my dad's question to answer mine instead. "I didn't want you to worry about how he was gonna react to you and me being together. Stress isn't good for you, baby. You're still recovering from a concussion."

"What the fuck is going on here?" Dad glared at Fox. "I thought Dahlia got caught in the crossfire of something with your club while she was here to see her sister."

I bit my bottom lip, then heaved a deep sigh of relief when my mom came inside the clubhouse with Molly. She was the only person who knew how to handle him when he was pissed. And judging by the look on his face, he was not happy to learn that another of his daughters had fallen for an Iron Rogue.

"How're you feeling, my sweet baby girl?" my mom asked as she rushed to my side. "Should you be up and around already? Maybe you should go lie down."

"I'm fine, Mom. Really," I assured her with a soft smile. "Just a headache, but I took something for that this morning."

"Not just a headache," Fox growled. "You have a motherfucking concussion."

Planting my fists on my hips, I glared up at him. "You two better not try to gang up on me. You heard Blade. He said that I didn't have to stay in bed."

"He also said not to tire yourself out," Fox grumbled, nudging me toward one of the couches. "At least sit down. For me. Please."

"And me," my mom added.

I dropped onto the cushion with a huff. "There, happy?"

Fox perched on the arm of the couch, resting his hand on my shoulder. "Thank you, baby."

"Yes, thank you." My mom sat down next to me, with Molly on the other side. "You look better than I expected. I was so scared when your dad told me that you were hit by flying debris from a car bomb."

"It really does sound worse than it actually was," I assured her with a soft smile. "At least for me since I was knocked out. Fox had the hardest time since he had to see me like that and was stuck waiting for me to wake up without knowing if I would be okay."

My dad crossed his arms over his chest and glared at Fox. "Now that my wife is satisfied that my daughter will be okay, how about you tell me what the fuck is going on here?"

"I've claimed Dahlia as my old lady," Fox announced.

My dad's gaze dropped to the leather vest I was wearing, and his eyes widened. "Fucking shit. I didn't even have enough time to realize she was still in the United States and not flitting around Europe with friends so she could avoid my wrath, and you made her your old lady already?"

"Yup, I sure as fuck did," Fox confirmed with a smirk.

Leaning against Fox's leg, I beamed a smile at my dad. "You only have yourself to blame for your daughters throwing themselves into relationships at breakneck speed."

His brows drew together. "How in the hell is this my fault?"

"Because you surrounded us with a bunch of guys who claimed their women as soon as they found them," I explained. "Every story we heard growing up was basically love at first sight."

"Yeah, you normalized it," Molly added with a nod.

"In all fairness, we really did," Mom agreed, patting my thigh.

Dad switched his glare to her. "Is this what I have to look forward to with Callie? If so, she's never ever allowed to step foot on this damn compound. And none of the single members of the Iron Rogues can come to ours. No way in hell am I going through this again."

"Good luck with keeping her away when her nieces and nephews are going to grow up here," Mom pointed out.

"That better not happen any time soon," Dad grunted. "My girls are too young to be having babies."

My mom rolled her eyes. "They're years older than I was when I got pregnant with Molly."

Molly cleared her throat, and Dad's gaze zeroed in on her. "Holy hell, please tell me the bastard didn't knock you up already."

"I sure as fuck did," Maverick boasted.

"Fucking hell," Dad muttered while Mom cheered and gave my sister a hug.

"A grandbaby? That's wonderful news," she cried.

"I blame you for all of this." Dad pointed at Fox.

"Keep your single men away from the rest of the Silver Saint princesses."

Fox shook his head. "Not sure that's possible."

Dad's eyes narrowed as a muscle jumped in his jaw. "You tryin' to tell me you can't control your men?"

"No." Fox lifted my hand and pressed a kiss against the knuckle of my ring finger. "But if Dahlia wants a big wedding with all of her family there, I'm assuming that'll include your men's daughters since she grew up with them. And my club is the only family I have besides my dad, so they'll be there too."

"Well fuck," my dad groaned, raking his fingers through his hair.

"Married?" I tilted my head back to stare up at Fox.

His eyes burned into mine as he said, "Having my property patch on your back isn't enough for me, baby. I want my ring on your finger, my baby in your belly, and my mark inked on your skin."

"You do?" I gasped.

"Of course, baby. I love you so damn much, I'm not sure it'll stop there," he warned. "I might come up with other ways to claim you."

"You won't get any complaints from me." I sniffled. "Because I love you so damn much too."

Leaning toward me, he pressed a finger under my chin so he could claim my mouth in a deep kiss. One that didn't last nearly as long as I would've liked since my dad loudly cleared his throat to interrupt us. I reluctantly turned toward him and giggled at the look of resignation on his face.

"A grandbaby and a wedding." My mom clapped. "My day turned from the absolute worst to the very best."

Fox's breath was hot against my ear as he whispered, "I think we can make her week even better if I managed to score her a second grandchild that's due shortly after your sister is expecting Maverick's baby."

He was successful in his mission...we found out only one week later that I was also pregnant.

EPILOGUE

FOX

"Merry Christmas, baby," I whispered to Dahlia, rolling over so my body covered hers.

Her lips curled up as she opened her eyes and gazed at me sleepily. "Merry Christmas."

"Are you ready for your first present?"

She grinned and wrapped her legs around my waist. "If it involves an orgasm, then absolutely."

I chuckled and ran my hand down over her breast and the swell of her stomach to cup her pussy. "That's present number two."

"I beg to differ," she moaned, raising her hips to press my hand tighter against her center.

Grinning, I took my hand from between her legs and tweaked one of her nipple rings. "I love how fucking horny you are when you're pregnant, but I promise, it'll be worth the wait."

She pouted but didn't protest when I pushed myself up and twisted so she could see the back of my left shoulder. There had been an empty patch of skin there, but it was now etched with ink. I'd had Molly create a design based around a dahlia, with her name intertwined, but leaving plenty of room to add our kids' names. Molly completed it last night so I wouldn't have to hide it from Dahlia.

Maverick hadn't been happy to give her up or that I was keeping her up late when she was in her third trimester, but Molly was so excited about it that she convinced him to back off. Although he'd spent the entire time brooding in the corner of her station at Iron Inkworks.

She gasped. "Is that...?"

I glanced down to see her swallowing hard and tears welling up in her eyes.

"No tears," I grunted. I hated it when she cried.

"Then don't do sweet shit to make me swoon!" she snapped. Her mood swings had worsened now that she was almost seven months pregnant. I thought it was cute but didn't tell her because it just pissed her off.

"Do you like it?"

"It's...I love seeing my brand on you." Her tone was thick with desire, and her pussy glistened with arousal. I faced her again, but instead of stretching out over her, I moved down to lay between her thighs.

"It's time for your second present," I growled before I ate her for breakfast, then gave her a screaming orgasm with my cock buried deep into her pussy.

My girl was loud as fuck in bed, and I loved hearing her, so I'd been relieved when we moved into a house I'd built on the compound, a short walk from the clubhouse. I didn't have to keep her quiet anymore, and since she couldn't get enough of my cock these days, I got to hear every little moan and shout of ecstasy.

"I'd say that was a gift for us both," Dahlia teased as she softly glided her hands up and down my back.

"Then I guess we don't need to exchange any other presents."

She frowned and smacked my shoulder. "Not funny."

It cracked me up that she was so giddy about Christmas, which was the only reason I let her talk me into hosting a party at the clubhouse on Christmas Day.

"Come on, baby. We need to get shit ready for the shindig today. And I have a pile of shiny presents waiting under our tree." I meant that literally since I'd cajoled Molly into wrapping Dahlia's presents so they looked pretty and festive. They sure as hell wouldn't have looked good if I'd attempted to do it myself.

After opening our gifts, we showered—which took a lot longer since I fucked her against the wall under the hot spray—and dressed before walking over to the clubhouse.

Tank's old lady and some of the prospects' girl-friends bustled around the kitchen, working on the food. Dahlia offered to help, but before I could tell her no, Sheila tsked and shooed her away.

"Go relax and put your feet up."

I jerked my chin at Sheila, silently thanking her, and she beamed back at me. She'd been ecstatic to learn she wasn't the only old lady around anymore. Tank was ten years older than me and had prospected when my dad was president. He and Sheila had been together since high school and married shortly after. For a while, there had been several other old ladies, but the old-timers who had wives or girlfriends had been phasing out of the life, retiring and moving to Florida and shit like that.

Sheila owned a small shop in town that sold wedding and formal dresses, so she'd been more than happy to put her sewing skills to use by making Molly's and Dahlia's property vests. She was also a fantastic cook.

"I'll bring you a little snack in a few minutes," she told Dahlia with a wink. My woman's eyes lit up, and I smiled as I led her out to the common room and settled her on the couch with a blanket and her e-reader.

A few minutes later, Maverick came down from his room and talked his pregnant old lady into joining mine.

"How's it going with the plans for the new house?" I asked as we watched our wives whisper to each other and giggle. Maverick had surprised Molly by buying an empty lot in Iron Rogues territory a couple of months ago, and their home was currently being built.

"Molly is having fun picking everything out. I'm just anxious for it to be done and for us to have our own space."

"I get it." My home had been done before his because I was the president, so it had been prioritized.

The front door opened, and a gust of chilly wind

swept through the room. It was a colder winter than usual for southern Tennessee. I glared at Dahlia's dad as he ushered his old lady inside, followed by his two youngest kids.

"Just because your daughters are married to the prez and VP doesn't mean you can just barge in anytime you want." Mac had unexpectedly "dropped by" a few times since I'd been with Dahlia. I highly doubted his claims that he had business in the area and suspected he was checking to make sure his girls were being treated right. Not that I blamed him. I'd probably do the same with my daughters. But that didn't mean I wasn't going to give him shit over it.

"He was invited, Kye," Dahlia sighed as she hopped up from the couch to hug her mother.

I grumbled but didn't bait her dad any further since I'd promised my wife that I'd get along with him at the party.

He'd made no such promise, though, so he pricked at my patience endlessly throughout the shindig. By the time everyone left, my jaw ached from grinding it all day to hold my tongue.

Dahlia owed me, and I fully intended to collect.

When we sat down to eat our Christmas dinner, we were startled by the back door banging against the wall as it was shoved open. Storm stumbled in, carrying a woman in his arms. "Blade!" he shouted. "Need your help. Now!"

Blade jumped up from his spot at the table and rushed over to Storm, taking the shaking woman from him. He froze for a second as he stared down at her, shock washing over his face before his expression became one I was very familiar with. Then he glanced at Storm and grimaced.

"Clinic," he grunted before turning and stalking down a hall that led to his medical office.

Dahlia leaned toward me, a frown on her gorgeous face. "Did I just see Blade struck by Cupid's arrow?"

I rolled my eyes at her expression but nodded in confirmation.

"That's great!" She smiled, then her brow drew down in confusion. "Why did that make him mad?"

"Because of who she is," I answered. Chuckling, I silently wished Blade good luck with that complication. Suddenly, my situation with Dahlia's dad didn't seem so bad.

"Well?" Dahlia huffed when I didn't continue. "Who is she?"

I grinned and shook my head. "Storm's little sister."

"I SHOULD KEEP you on the brink of coming for as long as I had to put up with your dad today," I grunted as I gently pushed Dahlia's torso down so she was holding her weight on her forearms with her delectable ass high in the air.

She was dripping down her thighs from being teased for the last half hour. I'd worked her to the edge, then let her fall back before doing it again. Over and over.

"Please, Kye," she pleaded, her voice ragged and her breathing choppy.

"Keep begging me, baby. Don't think I didn't notice you teasing me all day, either." Dahlia had stolen touches whenever she could, sometimes even pressing her hand against my dick for a moment as she walked by. She'd looked at me with a sly smile over her shoulder when she wiggled her ass while sitting on my lap. When I set her beside me to avoid coming in my pants in the middle of the lounge with our family all around, she'd let out a tiny whimper and squeezed her legs together. It had taken all my strength not to drag her upstairs and fuck her.

I slapped my palm down on one of her pale ass cheeks, and heat shot to my dick at the sight of the red handprint I left behind. "You were a naughty girl today, Dahlia." I smacked the other cheek and smiled smugly when she tried to hold in her moan. She was very adventurous in bed, so I hadn't been shocked the first time I made her come just by spanking her and petting her pussy.

She was a delicious mess between her thighs by the time I'd made sure she'd feel her punishment every time she sat down tomorrow.

I ran two fingers through her folds, then brought the sticky digits to my mouth and licked them clean. "So damn sweet," I murmured.

"Kye. I can't take any more. Please, fuck me."

Slipping my hands under her torso, I cupped her big tits and pulled her up so her back was against my chest. I rubbed my long, fat cock against her ass and plucked at her nipple rings as I whispered in her ear. "Gonna fuck you so hard, your pussy is gonna be just as sore as your ass tomorrow. Want you to feel me every time you move and remember what happens when you tease me."

She moaned and reached back to plunge her fingers into my hair. "Yes," she cried out.

"Who owns you, baby?"

"You," she panted.

I glided one hand down to her center and

cupped her, pushing two fingers inside her channel. "Who does this pussy belong to?"

She shuddered and moaned. "Ohhhh, yesss."

"Whose pussy is this, baby?" I snapped before giving her sex a sharp slap.

"You!" she shouted. "It's yours! Can I come now?"

I positioned my cock at her entrance and grabbed her hips before driving my cock deep inside her, sheathing myself completely and bumping her cervix. "Fucking hell. Swear you've gotten tighter since I knocked you up." I moved my hands to her belly and cupped the swell as I began to pump in and out of her slick heat. "So fucking good," I groaned. "Love the way you take my cock so damn deep. That's it, baby, squeeze me. Oh, fuck yeah."

"More," she wheezed, digging her fingers into my scalp. The slight bite of pain sent a zing of pleasure straight to my dick, and I had to work to force back my climax.

"My baby wants it rough?"

She nodded frantically and clenched her inner muscles, shattering my control. "Need you, Kye. Yes! Harder! Oh yes! Yes! Don't stop!"

I couldn't even if I tried. My hands slid over her silky skin, up to cup her tits, and I massaged the mounds as I thrust in and out of her. "Love these tits," I rasped. "Gonna fuck 'em later. After I fuck your pussy raw."

Dahlia arched her back, pressing her breasts into my hands as I tugged on her piercings, hissing when her inner muscles spasmed around my shaft. The beast inside me took over, and I pushed her back down before clutching her hips in a bruising grip. I yanked her back each time I slammed my hips forward. The sound of our sweaty skin slapping together heightened my raw need.

"Yes! Yes!" Dahlia threw her head back and clenched the sheets in her fists as she cried out.

"Fuck, baby. Oh fuck. Take it! Fuck my cock! Fuck, yes! Oh fuck!"

I slapped each ass cheek twice, then filled her one last time, going as deep as possible before my release whipped through me, and I roared her name.

The second my hot seed splashed into her womb, Dahlia screamed, and her pussy rippled around my member as orgasm rocked her body.

When I caught my breath and managed to think a little clearer, I held her against me as I maneuvered us onto our sides, staying connected with my dick sheathed inside her and my arms around her.

"Love you, baby," I said softly. "Merry Christmas."

"Very merry indeed," she sighed with a giggle. "Love you, too, Kye."

We lay there in silence for a while, enjoying the afterglow. Then Dahlia turned her head so she could look up at me. "I have one more present for you."

I raised an eyebrow and waited, trying not to laugh at the adorable twinkle in her pretty green eyes.

"I had an ultrasound today. We're having twins."

EPILOGUE

DAHLIA

"Are you ready to get your ears pierced, sweetie?"

Violet did a little celebratory dance, punching her fists in the air as she squealed, "Yes!"

"Are you sure you want to do this?" Fox asked.

"Uh-huh," Violet chirped with a nod. "I've been ready forever."

Our oldest daughter could be dramatic at times, but she wasn't exaggerating at the moment. She'd been asking for this ever since she was two.

Since she was a tiny baby, Violet had always been fascinated with the piercings in my ears. Which I found ironic since I had ended up taking out the barbells in my nipples the entire time I was breastfeeding her and Jett. Although it was safe to keep in piercings between feedings, having twins meant that it felt as though one baby or the other was always on my boob. It just hadn't been worth the effort of taking them off and putting them back on again every hour of the day. Especially when I was barely getting any sleep.

Fox was a fantastic father, but having two infants at the same time had been rough. Even when my parents had come to help for the first two weeks... much to my husband's dismay since he wanted to keep the babies and me all to himself. Although he ended up being grateful for the help after a few sleepless nights.

Thank goodness, none of our other pregnancies had been multiples. After having twins, each additional baby seemed easy in comparison.

"You're only ten," Fox grumbled.

Violet planted her little fists on her hips and glared up at her dad. "Yeah, and that's when you said I could finally get my ears pierced."

"I didn't mean the first thing the morning of your birthday."

Our daughter pressed her hands together and puffed out her bottom lip. "Please, Daddy. The last time I went to watch Mom work, I even picked out the pair of earrings I wanted her to use. This is the present I want the most for my birthday."

I knew how possessive Fox could be when I married him, so I hadn't been surprised when he'd put his foot down about my piercing. As long as I wasn't doing dicks, tits, or pussies, he was cool with me working at Iron Inkworks. Assuming that any male client was connected to the club.

After what had happened with Molly and her stalker, I couldn't even tell him that he was being ridiculous because all he had to do was remind me of the man who'd put a gun to my sister's head.

Not that we argued about it much since I was happily busy taking care of my family—the one that was just Fox's and mine and the one I'd gotten by becoming the old lady to the president of the Iron Rogues. But I still kept up my skills by popping into Iron Inkworks from time to time. And my daughter loved spending time with me while I was there. I wouldn't be even the tiniest bit surprised if she decided to follow in my footsteps, over her father's protest just like it'd been with mine.

Luckily, today's battle over getting her ears pierced was only a small one. Fox was a man of his word, and he hated disappointing his baby girls. So he nodded with a sigh. "Okay, if that's what you really want, then I guess we can head over to Iron Inkworks before going downtown to the diner for breakfast."

"Can I get two orders of cinnamon apple French toast?" Jett asked as he wandered into the kitchen, raking his fingers through his tousled hair.

"Absolutely," I agreed with a smile. "It's your birthday. You can get their extra-special hot chocolate to go with it if you'd like."

His eyes widened. "With the whipped cream, sprinkles, marshmallows, and cotton candy on top?"

I nodded. "Yup."

"Awesome!"

"But not until after Mom and I are done piercing my ears," Violet reminded.

"Which we're going to do right now." I slipped on my shoes and quirked a brow at my husband. "Can you get everyone ready to head to the diner? This shouldn't take long."

"Yeah." He still didn't look happy as he brushed his lips against mine and whispered, "Take care of our baby girl."

"Always."

He pulled his cell phone from his jeans and tapped out a quick text. "One of the prospects is gonna give you two a ride there and back."

I shook my head with a sigh. "It's only two blocks away."

"It's either that, or you wait until everyone's ready to head downtown, and we make it a family trip to Iron Inkworks for all of the kids to watch Violet get her ears pierced."

When he put it that way, it was easy to agree. "A ride there sounds great, but how about you just pick us up as soon as you get the rest of our children corralled."

"Sure, I can do that, baby." He gave me another quick kiss. "See you soon."

It usually took the kids a full hour to get dressed and ready to head out the door, but he must've rushed them along because they showed up a few minutes after I finished Violet's piercings. She was busy twisting her head back and forth to stare at them in the mirror and barely noticed when her dad stopped behind her to tell her how pretty they looked.

"How'd it go?" he asked when I sidled up to him and laced our fingers together.

I knew he'd been worried about her being in pain, even if only for a second or two. "She did great."

"Our babies are growing up too fast," he

complained.

Tilting my head back to smile up at him, I whispered, "Don't worry, you'll have another one in the nursery in about seven months."

Want to know what happens with Blade and Storm's sister? Find out in Blade!

Curious about Nic DeLuca? Read about how he fell for Gianna in The Mafia Boss's Nanny!

In the mood for another age gap romance? If you join our newsletter, we'll send you a FREE ebook copy of The Virgin's Guardian, which was banned on Amazon!

ABOUT THE AUTHOR

The writing duo of Elle Christensen and Rochelle Paige team up under the *USA Today* bestselling Fiona Davenport pen name to bring you sexy, insta-love stories filled with alpha males. If you want a quick & dirty read with a guaranteed happily ever after, then give Fiona Davenport a try!

For all the STEAMY news about Fiona's upcoming releases... sign up for our newsletter!

Printed in Great Britain
by Amazon